Tales　T

95 Good Puppy and Evil Kitten

Nice puppy. Cute baby. And the evillest kitten in the world.

114 H & G and the Witch's Cottage

If your step-parents don't want you, they can always sell you to a sweet-looking grandma who cooks a lot of gingerbread.

132 The Wolf's Party

When Baby Human's parents take him to a party at Wolf Manor, they can't understand what all the fuss is about. Surely everybody plays 'Put the Pig in the Cooking Pot' at parties?

145 Davy and the Trolls

They know where you live, and they're coming to get you.

Note to the reader:

These stories are brilliant for reading out loud. Tell them to your little brother, your Grandma or your dog. Even better, get your dog to read them to your little brother while your Gran makes you a mug of hot chocolate.

But whether you read them in your head or tell them out loud to your hamster, _you need to do the voices_. Just go for it! Make Bad Santa sound like a pirate, and make the Easter Bunnies talk like the cool bandits they are. Make the Sharks sound hungry. Make the Evil Kitten sound like he has an Evil Plan (he has).

I've included a guide to the voices for each story. However, these are only _my_ ideas, and there's no reason why the troll in your head should sound exactly like the one in mine...

Other books by Ed Wicke:
Wicked Tales
Wicked Tales Two: Even Wickeder Tales
Billy Jones, King of the Goblins
Akayzia Adams and the Masterdragon's Secret
Akayzia Adams and the Mirrors Of Darkness
Mattie and the Highwaymen
Bullies
Nicklus
The Muselings
Screeps

Ed Wicke

Wicked Tales Three:
The Witch's Library

With thanks to all those who encouraged me while I wrote & tried out these new stories... but especially:

... Patrick Wright, my patient and understanding boss.

... The children and teachers who have let me try out my stories on them, given me advice and helped me become a better writer: Kerry Mistry (née Thomas) and Westfields Junior School, Yateley; Karen Lang and Robert Sandilands Primary School, Newbury; Karen Sewell and Charles Kingsley's CE Primary School, Eversley; Sally James and Kingsclere CE Primary School.

Published by BlacknBlue Press UK
13 Dellands, Overton, Hampshire, England
blacknbluepress@hotmail.com

Ed Wicke (edddwicke@hotmail.com)
Tom Warne (tom@tomwarne.co.uk)
Janine Douglas
Rob Wicke
Rachel Wicke Eggington
Steve Eggington
David Eggington (4 years)
Rob Wicke
Sally Rose
Alice Wicke McKinstrie
Ben McKinstrie
Ara McKinstrie (16 months)
Dorothy Wicke

ISBN 978-0-9840718-2-1

It All Starts

Robbie tried to get to sleep but couldn't. The voices were keeping him awake.

At first he thought it was just the television in Aunt Mildred's room. But he kept hearing his Aunt's voice, and a child's voice answering.

He crept from his room and along long, gloomy corridors, avoiding the three creaky floorboards.

He tiptoed to his aunt's bedroom door and listened at it, but couldn't make out what she was saying. Then he heard the other voice, the voice of a frightened young girl: crying, pleading, miserable.

He couldn't bear it. And though afterwards he realised it was a foolish thing to do, he turned the doorknob and walked into his aunt's room.

'You *stupid* child!'

Robbie didn't dare look up. His eyes were fixed on his bare feet. She was right; he was stupid. When he had entered the room, she was sitting up in bed reading a book, while the television gabbled in a corner. That was all.

'Sorry,' he said. 'I was – I was scared.'

'Never enter my room without knocking! *Never!*'

'Sorry.'

'Do I have to lock my door? In my own house? *Look at me!*' she shouted.

He looked up and saw short black hair, thin red lips and green eyes that were cold and hard. 'Sorry,' he repeated.

'Get back to bed. You - *waste of space!*'

He went, thinking he must have imagined the voices – and imagined them last week as well. He climbed back into bed, miserable, thinking that Aunt Mildred hated him.

But then he thought: *It's not just me. She hates all children.* Aunt Mildred was a children's librarian at the big library in town, but she hated children! This thought made him laugh, and he had to muffle the laugh with a pillow.

At least she didn't *pretend* she liked children. Some of Aunt Mildred's friends were like that, all smiles and special friendly voices they put on for children. But you could tell it was an act, and that was even worse.

Robbie fell asleep thinking about it.

It was another week before he heard the voices again: Sunday evening, just like before. He ignored them now; it must be a weekly television program.

Then the doorbell rang twice and he heard his aunt run downstairs to answer it. There were voices in the lower hallway. His aunt came back up the stairs, switched off the television, banged a few cabinets and then went downstairs again. He heard the front door shut. Then silence.

It wasn't the first time she had dashed out late at night. He nearly turned over and went back to sleep, but an odd thought popped into his head:

Go and see.

He lay still for a minute longer. The three words went round and round in his head. They were getting smaller and smaller, whispering now, almost fading into nothing.

But just as he felt himself falling to sleep, he suddenly decided. And he was down the corridor in a flash.

 At first, he was disappointed. There was nothing. Just his aunt's duvet folded back and a drawer half-open.

Then he looked up at the bookshelf above the bed, where there were seven black books in a row. He was about to climb onto the bed and take one down when he noticed the corner of an eighth book poking out from beneath the duvet, with an oddly shaped pen clipped to the cover.

He lifted the book carefully and studied it. No title anywhere. No author, either. Just a black leather cover.

The pen clipped to the cover was black and shaped like a snake, with tiny green stones for eyes. Aunt Mildred had two weird pens like that, and he wasn't allowed to touch them. He left this one alone and opened the book.

The title page was handwritten:

Little Red Riding Hood
by Mildred Wiccover

Robbie stared at it. His aunt was writing books! That might explain her anger when he had burst in on her. And the voices, too: maybe she was saying the stories out loud.

He knew he ought to put the book back and return to his room. It was none of his business. He was *snooping*. But he was filled with curiosity now. He *had* to know.

He turned the page.

There was a picture opposite the first chapter, of a plump young girl in a red hooded cloak, with blond hair spilling out. She had a basket on one arm and was hurrying through some woods. She looked happy.

'I don't suppose she's happy for long,' Robbie said out

loud, recalling the story of Red Riding Hood and the Wolf.

'I'm not,' the girl said, looking up at him from the picture.

Robbie dropped the book. He waited a few seconds, then picked it up and opened it again to the chapter page.

The girl was still looking out of the book: looking for him. She asked, 'Are you real? You *seem* like an ordinary boy.' She lisped a little, saying "weal" instead of "real" and "theem" instead of "seem".

'I'm Robbie,' he said.

'I'm Bwenda. Or - I *was*. Has she caught you, too?'

Robbie didn't know what the girl was talking about. He opened his mouth to reply, then closed it again.

'Oh, *I* thee,' she said dismissively, lisping more than ever. 'It's jutht another game, is it? Twying to twick me with thomeone pwetending to be weally, weally thtupid?'

'What? You're calling me stupid?' asked Robbie.

'I didn't have to,' she said. 'You did it yourself when you stared at me with your mouth open like a goldfish.'

'What are you talking about?' he asked. 'I just opened my aunt's book and –'

'I don't believe you!' she shouted. 'As soon as I relax and think it's going to be okay this time, he'll leap out and –'

The girl covered her face with her hands and began to cry. Her shoulders shook.

Robbie tried to put his hand on her shoulder, but she was just a drawing in a book and his hand was as big as the whole picture. She shrank back from the huge shadow of his hand approaching.

'Sorry,' he said, pulling his hand back. 'I'm not – whatever you think I am. I'm just a boy. Aunt Mildred is my mother's sister. I heard voices and –'

But the girl had put her head to one side, listening. Her face had gone pale.

'She's coming!' the girl said softly. 'You'd better go.'

Then Robbie heard it too: the front door closing.

The girl whispered up to him again: 'Save yourself! It's too late for me!' She turned and ran off into the woods.

Robbie didn't know what to do. Then he heard his aunt's footsteps on the stairs and fear took over. He slid the book back under the covers and fled.

It wasn't until he got back to his room that he discovered he was holding the snake pen in his hand. He hid it under his pillow and got into bed quietly. When his aunt looked in a few minutes later, he appeared to be sound asleep.

A tricky situation

Robbie's world had fallen apart shortly after his twelfth birthday. His mother had become very ill, and his father hadn't been able to cope with looking after both her and Robbie: so Robbie went to live with Aunt Mildred.

Mildred had never got on with Robbie's mother - *and* she didn't like children - but she was the only relative they had. Besides, she had a big house in London and lived near to a good school. So she took Robbie in, along with one suitcase of clothes and a few books.

'No toys!' Aunt Mildred had insisted. 'I'm not having noisy cars and balls and guns in my house!'

She was ten years older than her sister and totally unlike her. Robbie's mother was kind and gentle, and liked nothing more than spending a weekend having fun with her one child; Aunt Mildred however was clever, brisk and unyielding. She did laugh, but usually about things Robbie didn't understand at all.

But it won't be for long, Robbie kept telling himself. His mother would recover and then everything would go back to normal. Until then, he would do the one thing his mother had asked him to promise: he would try not to annoy Aunt Mildred too much.

He was trying not to annoy her now, as he got up with the

alarm and made his own breakfast. He washed, dressed and was ready for school before she could shout for him.

He thought about the book all week. It was a *mystery*. He liked mysteries and when he went to the library he usually borrowed one to read. Unfortunately, this was the library where his aunt worked, so she saw the books he chose and always said they were stupid.

Robbie watched her carefully all week. She was the same as ever: happy in her own way, but certainly not happy with him. He had the impression that she was watching him, too.... Maybe she had missed the pen? He was still waiting for a chance to put it back in her room and carried it around in his pocket, wrapped in some tissues.

When Saturday came, he couldn't concentrate on anything except The Book. So when Aunt Mildred popped out "for an hour" he ran to her room, stood on her bed and took down the book on the far right side of the shelf. He sat on the bed and opened it with fingers that trembled.

'*You're back!*'

The girl Brenda couldn't contain her joy. 'I just *knew* you would come back!' she exclaimed. 'And you'll let me out, won't you? Pleathe?' she lisped. (*And after this, I won't usually mention her lithping*).

Robbie realised that his mouth was hanging open again and he made an effort to say something sensible. 'I'll try,' he said. 'But I'm not sure what to do.'

'Tear the page out?' suggested Brenda.

He nodded and tugged at the page with the picture on it. She screamed.

'Sorry,' he said. Brenda had fallen to her knees and was clutching at her chest.

'Ripping me in two...' she whimpered. 'That hurt *so* much. How *could* you?'

'It was your own idea!' Robbie said scornfully. 'Maybe I

should use scissors instead.'

He ran to find some. Then he tried to snip out the page, following close to the binding of the book. But Brenda screamed again, and he saw blood staining her dress.

'You're so *clumsy!*' she shouted up at him.

'I wasn't anywhere near you!'

'Doesn't matter,' she groaned. 'That won't work.'

He put the scissors on the bedside table. 'So – what now?'

Brenda sat down on a log. She reached into her basket and took out a chocolate cupcake which she shoved, whole, into her mouth.

'Baff's beffer,' she said with her mouth full. 'Muff beffer.'

'What?'

'Neeb foob. Ffate of ffock.'

'*What?*'

She swallowed the cupcake. 'I *need* food!' she explained. 'I'm in a state of shock, after being chopped to pieces by your *clumsy* scissor work.'

'Then I'm sorry I tried to help!' said Robbie angrily. 'I should have left you there!' He began to shut the book.

'Wait!' Brenda shouted. He paused and she continued grumpily, 'Okay, I shouldn't have said that. It wasn't your fault. But it *really* hurt.'

Robbie took a deep breath and counted to ten. 'Apology accepted,' he said. 'So… what next?'

'I don't know,' she said.

'I could tell the police.'

She laughed at him. 'Tell them *what?*'

'I don't know. But it's worth trying.'

He stood up. 'I'll have to do it now,' he said. 'Or else –'

But just then the bedroom door opened and his Aunt Mildred was in the doorway, with an odd smile on her face.

'Or else what?' she asked.

Into the Woods

Robbie turned to face his aunt and put the book behind his back. 'Sorry,' he said. 'I shouldn't have come into your room. I – I –'

Aunt Mildred shut the door behind her, and locked it. 'You were being nosy,' she said. 'As usual.'

Robbie turned red. It was true. He *was* a bit too curious for his own good.

'And now,' said his aunt quietly as she approached, 'now you pay the penalty. The book, please.'

Robbie gave it to her.

She opened it and turned it around so that Robbie was looking at the picture of Red Riding Hood.

'You want to know what happens next, don't you?' she asked. Her voice was soft, but full of poison.

Robbie said nothing.

'Perhaps she gets away this time. Perhaps not. You don't know until you get to the end of the story, do you?'

Robbie shrugged.

'The world is full of mysteries. You want to look into them all, don't you Robbie? You want to see everything, even the things you know you *shouldn't* see. Of course you do.'

Robbie was frozen, like a mouse hypnotised by a swaying snake – a black, twisted snake with glittering green eyes.

'So look in the book, Robbie. Look *deep* inside. Your curiosity is too strong for you – isn't it? You *must* see. You *must* find out what happens next.'

Robbie nodded. For a moment, it was true: he *must* know. He imagined that he would die of curiosity if he didn't know the end of the story.

Aunt Mildred laughed – a dry, confident laugh. 'And you

can know. Look... Look close... Look deep... *Look.'*

Robbie bent forward. The book was like the surface of a still lake. He could see beyond that shining surface, into the cool depths, where a fascinating little story was being acted out. He could scarcely make out the characters and their voices were so soft that he couldn't quite hear them. He *must* hear them. He leaned closer. His face broke the surface of the lake. The faces were coming into focus now. The voices were growing clearer.

And suddenly he was standing in the woods next to Red Riding Hood, and she wasn't happy with him.

'You – *idiot!'*

Red Riding Hood was crying again, but in anger this time. 'I could have got away!' she complained loudly. 'All you had to do was be *careful!'*

'Sorry,' said Robbie.

'Boys!' Brenda exclaimed. 'So – so – *useless!'*

Robbie wasn't taking this. 'Just a minute,' he said. 'I didn't put you here. *I* was trying to get you out. Don't blame me for your own problems!'

'Well, it wasn't *my* fault!' the girl shouted. 'It was your stupid aunt's doing! I was just minding my business -'

There was a dry chuckle from the skies and they both looked up.

'You can't see her,' said Brenda. 'But you know she's there. You can hear everything.'

Robbie listened. The sounds of the house were all about them, but muted and distant, as if heard through water. The grandfather clock ticked, the television began to talk to it-self: but far away, unreachably far.

He calmed down and asked, 'What happened to you?'

'I was minding my own business in the library,' Brenda sniffed, tossing her head so that the pale gold of her long curls escaped from her hood and swirled about in the shadows of the wood. 'Then I glanced into the room next to me, and I saw a basket of warm cakes on the table inside.'

Robbie asked doubtfully, 'How could you tell they were warm by looking at them?'

She looked at him scornfully. 'I could tell by the smell of them, *stupid*. Anyway, I had to go and see. I *had* to!'

Robbie disagreed: 'No you didn't. No one *makes* you go into a room to look at cakes.'

'You wouldn't understand. Sometimes you just *need* a cake. Especially a warm one.... Besides, I'd already eaten the biscuits and crisps I'd brought. And your horrid aunt had taken away my bag of sweets because she said the wrappers made too much noise!'

'Okay, so you went and looked. And then?'

'It was an odd room,' said Brenda, making a face. 'I realised that I'd never noticed it before, even though I must have sat by it many times. It was shaped like a triangle, so that it got narrower for each step you took. There was beautiful wallpaper on the wall – covered with drawings of tall trees with thin, elegant branches and lovely shadows.'

Brenda sighed. 'I went up to the cakes. They were in a dear, old-fashioned wicker basket. They smelled of sunshine and honey and flowers and happy summer picnics in a meadow, and I just *had* to eat one.'

'You ate one of someone else's cakes?'

For the first time, Brenda looked embarrassed. 'I ate *all* of them,' she confessed. 'And when I'd gobbled the lot, I looked around and found that the door had disappeared and the wallpaper had turned into a real wood. The same wood we're standing in now.'

'Serves you right,' said Robbie. 'You shouldn't be so greedy.'

'Yeah? Well, it serves *you* right as well, then! *You* shouldn't be so nosy!'

They glared at each other.

Aunt Mildred's laughter came again. Robbie whispered to the girl, 'This is stupid. She likes seeing us fight.'

She whispered back angrily, 'Stop picking on me, then!'

Robbie almost replied just as angrily, but realised it wouldn't do any good.

'What's going to happen now?' he asked instead.

'Nothing,' said Brenda. 'It's not Sunday yet. She only makes up stories on Sundays. *Let's see what the Good Book says today,* she says. It's one of her sick jokes.'

'Does she read your story every Sunday, then?'

'No, she does each book in turn. She read mine last week, and she'll work her way along the line of books.'

'Oh,' said Robbie. 'You mean there are more stories... more children?'

'Of course. And she usually reads them in turn, though she sometimes skips one. She always goes from right to left, but I don't know why. It seems backward to me.'

'What's the next story about?'

Brenda said, 'A boy who sleeps a lot. There's something about Christmas in it, but I've never understood why.'

'And the next one?'

'I'm *bored* with your questions!' said Brenda haughtily. 'I'm not answering any more of them.' She sat down on a log and began eating a cake from the basket beside her. She stared off into the distance, ignoring him.

Robbie watched her for a while before whispering, 'But if we're going to escape, I need to know -'

'We're *not* going to escape,' she snapped. 'We *can't!* You wasted your one chance to save me, and now you're stuck here for ever and ever, or until she gets bored with us and puts us in the fire.'

Robbie sat beside the red-hooded girl and said, 'Sorry. I'm only trying to help. The stories my aunt makes up, are they the same each time? I mean, do you always make the same journey to Grandma's house, meet the same wolf, and...'

Brenda covered her face with her hands, sobbing. 'Oh, if only it *was* the same each time!' she moaned. 'She always changes it, always makes you hope that this time Grandma will have a gun, or you'll find a way home. But it always goes wrong. It *always* goes – goes –'

She had to stop because she was crying too hard.

'We'll escape,' said Robbie. 'We *will!* And then –'

But an evil laugh from beyond the wood stopped him. His aunt was still listening.

'We *will*,' he repeated in a whisper.

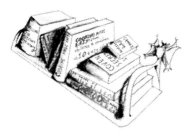

It should have been a pleasant afternoon – the little wood was warm and bright, with birds flitting through the trees – but Robbie didn't enjoy it much. He had to sit, bored, in the clearing with Little Miss Misery (as he had named her in his head). Brenda wouldn't explore the woods with him, and when he tried to do that himself, something odd happened.

'I don't get anywhere,' he said to Brenda after trying several times. 'I take a step into the wood, then find I'm walking straight back into the clearing.'

'Of *course* you don't get anywhere,' said Brenda in a superior voice. 'She hasn't written you into the story yet.'

'So I'm stuck here, in this page?'

'Yes – until she writes you in. But as soon as she does that, you'll wish you weren't born!'

'But why don't *you* go wander about the woods?' Robbie persisted. 'You might find a new path.'

'Why don't *I* wander about?' asked Brenda. 'You'll find out soon enough! Anyway, I'm going to sleep. Goodnight.'

She curled up in a patch of long grass and was asleep in a minute. Robbie looked up into the darkening sky and decided to sleep as well.

He thought at first that it would be impossible – but the

ground was oddly comfortable and the grass kept him warm somehow. He wondered for a moment whether there were ants and spiders crawling about, but as soon as he closed his eyes, he too was asleep.

The next day – Sunday - was as boring as the last, especially since Brenda didn't want to talk to him. She seemed worried, and kept glancing up at the sky.

As night fell, he could hear his aunt moving about in the bedroom, changing into her nightgown, putting on the television, then climbing into bed.

A hand appeared in the starry sky. It hesitated, seemed to pass them by, then came back, hovering above them.

'No!' whispered Brenda. '*Please* no! It's *not* my turn! You read me last week!'

But the hand plucked the whole wood into the air and swirled it about, to land dizzily in a giant lap.

Once upon a time ...

The pen paused in midair. If he squinted his eyes, Robbie could just see the words hanging in the dark sky, with one of his aunt's snake-shaped pens beyond them.

He couldn't stop himself from feeling in his jacket pocket to check that he still had the pen he'd found in her room. For a moment he wondered whether he could bargain with his aunt: *I'll give you back your pen if you set me free.* But she would just laugh and take it from him.

The pen above them began to write....

The Witch's Story

Once upon a time, there was a greedy little girl and a nosy boy.
She was called Red Riding Hood and he was called Boy Blue.
They were walking through the woods one morning, arguing with
each other. Then out from the woods…

Out from the woods padded a wolf.

Robbie gasped. He hadn't realised how large a real wolf was, how savage, how frightening.

The darkness had rolled away and he was standing in sunlight. Brenda was behind him, holding onto his jacket, keeping him between her and the wolf. Robbie tried to pull free but Brenda was desperate and surprisingly strong.

The wolf strode forward, then leapt towards them. Brenda screamed and let go of Robbie, running off into the woods. Robbie felt hot breath and heard the snap of strong teeth; his right arm hurt terribly; somehow he pushed the wolf away and ran into the woods as well, following Brenda.

There followed an hour of cat-and-mouse, or rather boy-and-wolf. Sometimes Robbie thought he had escaped; but then he would hear the steady panting of the animal, the careful footfalls and the crackling of leaves; he would look about him, terrified, seeing nothing but trees and more trees; then the wolf would be upon him with a horrendous growl, slashing and biting.

Just as Robbie thought he could run no further, he saw a white cottage that stood in a clearing. It seemed to him the most heavenly place: calm, clean, solid, with a brook bubbling gently beside it. He fought off the wolf once more and sprinted out from the trees, jumped the brook, ran through the tidy garden filled with flowers, and fell upon the door, banging at it with his fists.

A sweet and ancient lady opened the door. Her knitting was in one hand, and a pair of small round eyeglasses was on her nose.

'Do come in, dear,' she said pleasantly. 'Little Red is here already. Kick your shoes off on the mat, there's a good boy. Once I've locked the door, I'll make us all a lovely cup of tea and toast some bread over the fire.'

From inside the house came Brenda's voice: 'Don't let him in! The wolf will come after him! *Keep the boy out!*'

Grandma looked back over her shoulder and said, 'You know the wolf will find us whatever we do, Red: we might as well carry on normally while we wait for him.'

Robbie took off his shoes and came into the house. It was the dearest, sweetest cottage he could have imagined, with flowers everywhere and lovely paintings hanging on the walls. A kettle was singing on the stove and there was a wonderful smell of fresh baked bread.

'Hi, Brenda,' he said, waving to the girl who was sitting in a huge armchair, looking grumpy.

'Go *away!*' she said crossly. 'Go away, and maybe he'll eat you instead, and leave me and Grandma in peace!'

Robbie thought about this. Maybe she was right. Maybe he should go, and make the wolf chase him. Maybe that would break the witch's story, and –

'You know that won't work, Red,' said Grandma. 'The wolf won't be satisfied with just a few bites of Boy Blue, especially since Blue here is rather skinny. And in any case, it would be unkind for us to make the boy suffer just so we could have a better chance of getting away. We should look after one another, shouldn't we?'

Red pouted at this.

Grandma poured them all some tea, and they ate slices of toast with honey. She was a cheerful granny and Robbie was soon laughing and joking with her. Even Brenda cheered up. They were about to start a card game when –

'What was that?' asked Brenda sharply.

'I think it was –' said Robbie.

'No!' shouted Brenda. *'No!'*

'Now dears,' said Grandma, 'don't panic. Red, you grab the poker from the fireplace. I've got my knitting needles. Blue can use the toasting fork. We'll hold off that big, bad wolf for as long as we can…'

… The next ten minutes were frightening and very, very messy. Robbie didn't like to think of them afterwards. But at least there *was* an afterwards. Once everyone had been well and truly eaten, Robbie and Brenda found themselves back in their little clearing. They ached all over and their hearts were pounding from sheer terror, but they were alive and didn't have a single scratch on them.

'That was *horrible!*' Robbie groaned.

'It was!' Brenda agreed. 'That was one of the worst!'

They looked at each other and laughed.

'You did all right,' said Brenda. 'You were quite good with that toasting fork.'

'He didn't like your poker, either,' said Robbie.

'Especially since it was still red hot from the fire!'

They laughed again.

'Your Grandma's great,' Robbie said.

'She's *our* Grandma now, not just mine,' said Brenda.

… And they were good friends from that moment onwards, because there's nothing like standing back to back and fighting off a ravenous wolf to bring you together.

'…. The problem,' said Robbie the next day, 'is how to get out of the book.'

'No,' said Brenda (Red Riding Hood, Little Miss Misery and fellow Wolf Battler). 'The problem is how to get past the wolf. Once we do that, we'll be fine.'

'Why?'

'When you got to Grandma's house, didn't you see the path that goes beyond it?'

'No,' said Robbie. 'I was too busy running!'

Brenda said, 'In the distance, the path leads through a long meadow, across a stream, and then out into your aunt's room. I used to stare at it from Grandma's window while we waited for the wolf to come. I could see your aunt's bed, the grandfather clock, the television and that painting of a horrible twisted face on the far wall. And sometimes I could see you there.'

Robbie asked, 'So if you could see the way out, why didn't you escape?'

'Idiot! I *tried*! But each time the wolf caught me.'

'The path might have been a trick anyway.'

Brenda tossed her head angrily. 'I know that! I'm not *stupid*, you know! But *maybe* it's not a trick. *Maybe* it's a way out that she can't block, and all she can do it make it difficult for us by putting the wolf in the way!'

Robbie nodded. 'Okay. You could be right. But *maybe* there's a better way.'

He put his hand into his jacket pocket, pulled out his bundle of tissues and unwrapped them to reveal the pen.

Brenda exclaimed, 'Oh! *Oh!* Is it really one of hers?'

'Yes. It was next to the book when I first picked it up. I didn't mean to take it... it just seemed to stick in my hand. And I couldn't let her see it after that, so I still had it hidden in my pocket when she caught me.'

Brenda touched the pen with a finger, and shivered. 'What are you going to do with it?' she asked.

'I'll write a new story. One that lets us out.'

Brenda's face was transformed. 'Yes!' she exclaimed joyfully. 'Can we do it now?'

Robbie hesitated. 'I'm not sure what to write,' he said.

Brenda said, 'Ask Grandma. She'll have some ideas.'

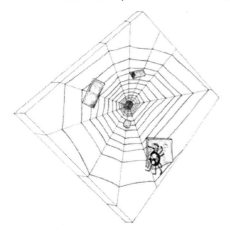

Robbie and Brenda went to opposite ends of their little clearing and began shouting for Grandma; within moments she popped out from the trees, her knitting wool catching at the branches as she tottered towards them. She sat on Brenda's log and asked what all the shouting was about.

'We're having a *very* important meeting,' said Brenda. 'We're going to work out how to get away.'

'What a lovely idea!' Grandma exclaimed.

There was a growl - and the Wolf strode into the clearing.

'Great idea,' he agreed, in a deep, resonant, refined voice. I'm bored with this place. Bored, bored, ***bored***.'

The children backed away from him.

'Oh, don't worry,' he said calmly. 'I can't eat you here. *That* story doesn't start until you're in the woods.'

'Don't trust him!' Brenda said to Robbie.

The Wolf snarled. 'Now *that* is exactly the attitude I *detest*,' he said. 'Narrow-minded, predictable, *boring*!'

'You must admit, though,' said Grandma, 'that you *do* eat us each time. *You're* predictable, too!'

The Wolf thought about this and said, 'I see your point. But who's the victim here? It's *me!* I should be out eating three little pigs and the occasional chicken. But what do I get? Under-ripe children and tough, stringy grandmothers!'

'You don't *have* to eat us!' said Brenda.

'Yes I do. It's in the story. I can't help myself.'

Grandma gave the Wolf a stern look and said, 'You don't try very hard to resist, do you, dear?'

The Wolf snarled at her. 'Resist? How?' he asked. 'The witch *makes* me do it. End of story. Literally!'

Robbie held up his pen. 'But look!' he said. 'We have a plan. We can rewrite the story. We can change it – and change the ending, too!'

The Wolf sat back on his haunches and thought for a bit. 'Okay,' he said. 'I'll go for that. But you can't turn me into a Nice Kind Wolf, or a Cute Kitten. That's so *dull!* You've got to use my full talents. I've had proper actor training, you know; been in lots of pantomimes. So here's the deal: you write me a story fit for a great actor, and I'll play it.'

'A funny story or a serious one?' asked Robbie.

The Wolf gave a superior sniff. 'In the theatre, dear boy, we call it *Comedy* and *Tragedy*. I've done a lot of tragedy, so I don't mind trying a comic part.'

'What story would you like, Grandma?' Robbie asked.

Grandma looked up from her knitting. 'I don't mind, dear,' she said, 'just so long as I don't get eaten. That's always rather messy and uncomfortable.'

'Right,' said Robbie. 'I'll make up something, and we'll all go along with it. Okay?'

Brenda glared at him. 'You haven't asked what *I* want!' she complained.

The Wolf gave a howling laugh and said, 'That's easy. Just stuff her full of junk food!'

Brenda fixed him with an evil

stare. 'I *need* food!' she said. 'No one understands that!'

Grandma looked at Brenda over her glasses. 'But the witch used food to catch you, dear. So maybe you should watch what you eat – until we get to the end of the story?'

Brenda bit her lip very hard. 'I'll try,' she said, 'so long as there aren't any chocolate cupcakes.'

'Okay,' said Robbie. 'No chocolate. And I'll make something special happen for you. I don't know what, yet....'

They looked at one another.

'I'm in,' said the Wolf. 'But it's got to be good. For a start, I think there should be some Bad Pigs in it. I'm tired of being in stories full of cute little piggies and big bad wolves.'

'I'm in, too,' said Brenda. 'But my part has to be better than Wolfie's.'

'Go for it,' said Grandma, counting her knitting stitches.

But they couldn't try it yet, because Aunt Mildred was at home with a cold all week, and spent most of the time in bed. Not Saturday or Sunday either, because she was home all day and kept coming into the bedroom. Then they had to listen while Aunt Mildred read a story on Sunday evening. The boy in the next book shouted and groaned as nameless horrors crawled about in the darkness, then screamed one last time and threw himself out of a window.

'He does moan an awful lot,' said Brenda, working her way through a box of chocolates. 'It can't be *that* bad.'

On Monday morning, as soon as Aunt Mildred had gone to work in the library, Robbie took up his pen and began to write upon the sky...

The Hood, the Wolf and the Evil Pigs

The voices

Red Riding Hood sounds young and sweet and does a lot of lithping (sorry - I mean lisping) but her voice is clear and confident and as she's as tough as nails. She's da main hood in da neighbourhood, know wot I mean, bro? She's gonna give dem pigs a deep fryin' lesson dey won't forget, like.

The **Wolf** has a big, furry, deep, proud, growly voice. He sounds tough and mean – and puzzled. He *knows* it isn't supposed to happen like this. He *knows* that little girls and grandmas ought to scream and then die in a spectacularly messy fashion. But you can tell he's actually quite pleased to give up grandma-gobbling; justice and revenge are **far** more important to him, so long as that involves eating a few tasty pigs.

Grandma is just like your own favourite Granny, except for the knuckle-dusters, tattoos and home-made ginger-chilli-curry-garlic throat medicine... or maybe your Gran **is** like that, in which case you and I must be related.

The **Pig** has a plump voice. Every word is round and fat. Every syllable oozes with greed. Every letter of every syllable is wet with pig slobber. Even the dot of every letter i is soaked in fat and sugar. He really thinks he has earned his bloated piggy banker's bonus, although he's as stupid as any pig... or any piggish banker.

The **Woodcutter** has done his job the same way for forty years - man and boy - and he's not going to change now. His voice sounds slow and stupid. When he isn't cutting down trees, he's at the pub telling other woodcutters why England didn't win the football World Cup.

The story

Once upon a time, there was a king who was so greedy that one day he turned into a pig, as did all the princes and princesses and most of their friends.

This didn't make much difference at first, except that extra food had to be delivered to the palace every day. But after a while, the pigs were having so many grand parties and building so many wonderful pigpen castles, that they ran out of money. The pig king's treasury was empty.

The evil, greedy pigs decided to open some special banks - Piggy Banks. Everyone in the kingdom had to put their money into these banks, and whenever the pigs wanted a few thousand – or millions – they just took out what the people had put in, and spent it on themselves.

The Piggy Bankers called this their Piggy Banking Bonus. 'We're worth it!' they snorted, and laughed until the tears ran down their fat, greedy cheeks.

As a result, the people became poor and sad. Some of them even lost their homes. But in their darkest hour, a hero arose...

Once upon a time in the deep dark wood
There lived a girl called RR Hood.
She wanted to do what a brave girl should:
Take from the bad and give to the good.
She set out one December's day
With plans to make those piggies pay
But out from the trees there prowled a beast
Looking for an early Christmas Feast.

The Wolf stepped out in front of Brenda
and howled at her, snarling and flashing his teeth.

'Gweetingth, Mister Wolf,' she lisped at him. 'I expect
you're wanting my bathket of lovely cweam caketh!'

'I want more than cakes!' he snarled.
'I'm the big bad wolf, you see:
The one they call the Wolf BB.
I eat little girls and grandmas, too.
And the bits left over, I make into stew!'

'Oh, goodie!' she exclaimed.

'What?' asked the Wolf - surprised that she was pleased to
see him, because normally *no one* is pleased to see a wolf.

Brenda said happily, 'You can take the cakes for me! That
will save me a lot of time, because it's Spring Cleaning day.
Here you are... One basket of cakes. One map showing the
way to Gwandma's house. One picture of Gwandma so you
can wecognise her. One passport with my name in it but
your picture in it so you can fool her into thinking you're
me. One tape recording of me saying "Hello Gwandma!" so
you can play it to her. One lovely Wwwred Hood to wear.
One wig to wear underneath it. There – you're all set!'

The Wolf took the basket and stood, puzzled, while RR
Hood loaded him with wig, hood and false papers. 'But –
but –' he began.

'Don't thank me!' exclaimed Red Riding Hood. 'Now I can
go and wob a few Piggy Banks before sunset and give the

money to poor children!'

... And in a moment she was gone.

The Wolf looked suspiciously at the cakes.

'Though I'm a wolf supremely bad
I now suspect that I've been had!
I'll have to change my evil plan
And make a sandwich out of Gran!'

He weaved his way through the wood, following the map that Brenda had given him. It led him straight to Grandma's dear, sweet cottage.

He paused outside the door and put on the wig and red hood. Then he banged the door knocker. An old lady voice called from within:

'Who's banging on my door so clear?
I hope you're not a wolf, my dear.
I'm old and frail and very sweet,
But I'll still kick you down the street!'

'It's me: Red Riding Hood!' the Wolf called.

The ancient voice replied, 'It doesn't sound like you, Brenda! My, what a big voice you have, Miss Hood!'

The Wolf played the recording of Brenda saying: *'Hello, Gwandma!'*

'Okay,' said Grandma, peering through a crack in the door. 'It *sounds* like you, but it doesn't *look* like Brenda. My, what a big nose you have, Miss Hood!'

The Wolf pushed his passport through the letter box. Grandma peered at it.

'Well, all right,' she said. 'You *are* Brenda. I expect it's just my memory playing tricks. You'd better come inside before you catch cold standing on the doorstep...'

She unlocked the door and let in the Wolf.

'Oooo – cakes!' she exclaimed, looking in the basket he held. 'And for once, you haven't eaten them already!'

She took the cakes from the Wolf's paw and walked away to put them in the kitchen. The Wolf leapt at her and bit her hard on the left leg.

'Owwwwwooooooooo!' he howled, holding his jaw.

Grandma stopped and looked back. '*Naughty* Brenda!' she said, wagging her finger at the Wolf. 'Trying to bite me on my wooden leg!'

She continued on her way to the kitchen, and the Wolf flung himself after her again, biting her right leg this time.

'Owwwwwooooooooo!' he howled, holding his jaw again.

'Now, now, Brenda,' she said calmly, 'you *know* I've got a steel brace on the other leg...'

She put the cakes on the side and set the kettle on the stove. The Wolf began to prowl towards her, growling.

'Brenda!' she said with some concern. 'That's a *very* bad cough you have! Let me find you some medicine.'

She took a large black bottle from the cupboard and poured a thick, greenish liquid onto a spoon. 'Now dear, open wide!'

The Wolf flung himself upon her, but she stepped deftly to one side and pushed the spoon into his mouth.

He stopped.

He wheezed.

He groaned.

He rolled over and over, howling.

'Really, Brenda,' said Grandma. 'Such a carry-on! Just like a little animal!'

The Wolf rolled to his front and tried to rise. 'That's – howwwwllllll! – arrrrrggggg – yowwowwoooo – *spicy!*' he moaned.

'Yes,' said Grandma. 'But it works wonders for coughs. Liquorice and chilli and garlic and pepper and cloves and a little curry powder.'

The Wolf licked his lips. 'It burns all the way down!' he groaned. 'And it's – it's... *amazing!* Can I have some more?'

'Of course,' said Grandma. 'But not until we've finished the cleaning. You remembered that it's Spring Cleaning to-day, didn't you?'

The Wolf howled. 'I don't like cleaning!' he complained.

'There, there, dear: it's not so bad,' Grandma said, tying

an apron around him and pushing a vacuum cleaner hose into his paw. 'Start on the carpet while I wash the dishes.'

The Wolf began pushing the vacuum cleaner around grumpily, muttering to himself. He watched Grandma from the corner of his eye, and when her back was turned he made a dash at her. But he got tangled in the vacuum cleaner cord and instead of biting her arm, he bit through the cord instead.

'*Yowwwwww!*' he groaned as the electricity surged through his jaws.

'What did you say, Brenda?' asked Grandma. 'Did you want a cookie and some milk?'

The Wolf pulled the cord from his mouth and nodded weakly.

After cookies and milk, he felt much better.

'Now, Wolfie,' said Grandma. 'What shall we do about Brenda?'

'But I *am* Brenda,' the Wolf insisted.

'No you're not,' Grandma said, sitting down and picking up her knitting. 'I know you're not Brenda, because Brenda has *never* brought me a whole basket of cakes. She always eats some of them on the way – usually *all* of them.'

'Talking about eating,' the Wolf growled, rising from the floor. '*It's dinner time!*'

Grandma pointed both needles at him. 'You're not having *me* for dinner, Wolfie!' she warned. 'But what would you *most* like to eat?'

Wolfie thought. He licked his lips. 'Sausages,' he said.

'Let's cook some sausages then,' said Grandma. 'Then we'll go help Brenda. She's *useless* at robbing banks!'

Just then there was a knock at the door. Grandma opened it and found a Woodcutter on the front porch.

'Uh,' he said stupidly, 'I was wonderin'... uh... maybe you've got a wolf you want choppin' up? I got my axe, see.'

He showed her his big axe.

'No thank you,' said Grandma. 'I'm quite fond of Wolfie

the way he is.' She shut the door.

Wolfie asked, amazed, 'What? Fond of *me*?'

'Of course,' said Grandma. 'You're a lovely wolf – except when you're eating people.'

'I do prefer sausages,' said Wolfie. 'Or roast ham.'

There was a noise from outside – the sound of a big axe chopping. Wolfie looked out the window and said:

'That Woodcutter is cutting down one of your trees.'

'Oh,' said Grandma. 'Is it the tall tree near the house?'

'Yes, the one that leans right over the house.'

She asked, 'You mean the one that will fall upon the house and crush us to smithereens?'

Wolfie growled, 'I'll go ask him to stop,' and went outside. There was a lot of shouting, growling and fighting; then Wolfie returned, carrying the axe in his jaws.

'He's gone now,' Wolfie said. 'And don't look at me like that: I only bit him a *little*.'

They ate sausage sandwiches and walked together through the woods towards the town. But they hadn't gone far before there was an odd sound behind them.

'That's a chainsaw,' said Grandma.

The chainsaw roared again, and then there was a loud cracking sound, and an even louder sound of smashing, crashing and crushing, as a big tree fell upon the house.

'Ah well,' said Grandma. 'I never liked that house any-way...'

Robbing banks

They went together through the woods to the town. Grandma and Wolfie began searching for Brenda.

'She'll be in the castle prison,' said Grandma. 'We'll have to rescue her.'

'How?' asked Wolfie.

Grandma took out her black bottle. 'First, we both take

some strengthening medicine,' she said. She gave them both a spoonful. 'And now we go kick some backsides...'

'Or bite them?' asked Wolfie hopefully.

They went to the castle and knocked politely on the door to the prison there.

There were three large soldiers waiting inside with swords and sticks and mousetraps. But they were no match for an angry grandma and a howling wolf. Soon the jail cell was unlocked and Red Riding Hood was running down the road with them.

They went into the nearest Piggy Bank and Brenda took her basket of cakes up to the desk, saying:

'I'm the one they call the Hood,
Come to make the poor feel good.
What I want is lots of money
To give to kids that haven't any.'

The bank manager – a finely dressed hog with polished hooves and a porkpie hat on his head - looked at her with his mouth open. 'What?' he grunted.

'Look,' said Red. 'It's really simple. I wish to swap these cakes for a basketful of money.'

'Large bills only!' added Grandma, pointing her knitting needles at the puzzled pig. 'Fifties and hundreds!'

'I'm sorry, ladies,' said the pig. 'We don't give money away. Especially not to crazy people.' He began feeling under his desk for the alarm buzzer, using one of his trotters.

Wolfie came out from behind Grandma and put his front paws onto the desk. He leaned over until his nose was touching the snout of the piggy bank manager. 'Fill the basket right to the top,' he growled, 'or I'll huff and I'll puff and sneeze all over you, and give you swine flu!'

'I – I – I -,' said the bank manager.

'Please?' Wolfie asked, showing his lovely, sharp teeth. 'We've got thousands of poor children to feed.'

'Certainly not!' exclaimed the pig tartly. 'I've *earned* all this money! I'd rather be turned into sausages than share it with anyone!'

Wolfie said, 'Hey - *great* idea! Piggy, you've got a deal!' And a minute later the basket was filled with money, and the pig was upside down in a big sack.

Soon they were running down the road towards the poorest part of town. When they got there, they posted the money through letterboxes and rang the doorbells.

Then they ran out of town, stopping at a café to swap a sack of pork for three orders of jumbo sausages and chips.

'Come on!' shouted Red. 'There's another Piggy Bank in the next town! We'll rob that one, too!'

Tuesday Night

Several bank robberies later, and after leaving a couple of heavy sacks at a butcher's, they met a boy sitting on a log, writing a story in a black book.

'Look!' said Robbie. 'I found this book here on the log. It already had most of the story, and I only needed to add the section about the banks and the food.'

'You write good sausages and chips,' said Red Riding Hood. 'I saved some of mine for you. I'm on a diet, see...'

'And we have some bacon crisps –'

'– hot dogs –'   ' – want a few Scotch eggs?'

'– and this crackling's great!' '– pickled trotters, anyone?'

Robbie joined them, and after robbing another bank, they walked right out the story into the hous...

    ...out of the story into...   *...out of the...*

'It's not working!' said Robbie.

'But I can see the room from here!' said Brenda.

'Try again!' growled Wolfie.

'It keeps erasing itself!' said Robbie.

This is a spotty hat by Davy

Grandma looked up into the sky, where the snaky writing was dissolving like a mist every time Robbie began it. She said, 'Perhaps you should use a more traditional ending.'

'Like *They all lived happily every after*?' puzzled Robbie. He tried that, but it didn't work either.

'Oh!' Brenda said. 'I know! *The End*!'

'Yeah, try that one,' Wolfie agreed.

Robbie wrote it carefully in the book he had in his hand. It stayed there, and the same words drifted across the sky.

Then everything went dark.

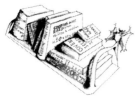 … They weren't in Aunt Mildred's room. But it was someone's bedroom somewhere, and the Someone was sleeping in a small bed, lit by a patch of moonlight.

There was a narrow window at one end of the bed and a large open fireplace at the other. Someone had built a barricade between the bed and the fireplace – a pile of books, cushions, pillows and cardboard boxes. It reached almost to the ceiling and looked likely to fall over at any moment.

The person on the bed woke, and sat up with a jolt. He held out his arms as if to fight off something and opened his mouth to shout – but stopped and stared instead.

'What are *you* doing here?' he whispered. He peered left and right into the half-darkness, as if expecting something to come out of it. He looked the nervous sort.

'I don't know,' said Robbie. 'I thought we would go through to my aunt's room. But I think we've gone from one story to the next instead.'

The boy stared at them again. He was small, thin, pale and dressed in striped pyjamas. 'What?' he asked.

Brenda asked in an exasperated whisper: 'Are you *crazy*? You've been in a book for months, or haven't you noticed?'

The boy peered at her. 'You lisp a lot,' he said. 'Are you the one I hear shouting and screaming, and complaining about a wolf all the time?'

'Yeth!' she shouted.

'Oh. So you've come into my story now. I hope you didn't bring the wolf with you!' The boy laughed uncertainly.

Wolfie stepped forward. 'Hi there!' he said.

The boy gasped and tried to hide beneath the covers. 'Hi,' his muffled voice called back weakly.

'He won't eat you,' Brenda promised.

'Not unless I get *really* hungry,' said Wolfie.

The boy sat up cautiously and looked around the room again. 'Is You Know Who here?' he asked.

'My aunt?' asked Robbie.

'No! *Santa!*' he breathed, looking terrified.

'I wish he was,' said Brenda.

'Don't say that!'

'Why not? Everyone loves Santa.'

The boy shook his head. 'They don't love *Bad* Santa. They don't love him when he comes down the chimney as a giant centipede and crawls around the room. They don't love him when he's covered in slime or has tentacles that suck the life out of you. You can't love Santa when he promises you the most wonderful and amazing presents, but all you get is a slug in your hot chocolate!'

'Yuk!' they all said.

'The nice Santa in the shopping centre promised me a new pair of glasses,' said the boy. 'Mine had broken, which is why I can't see you all properly. Anyway, he said "*Ho ho ho young Tom, consider it done!*". Then I was walking back past the library. I was so happy that I started skipping –'

'*Bad* mistake!' exclaimed Robbie. 'Aunt Mildred doesn't like skipping!'

'Or laughing out loud,' added Brenda.

'Or smiling at breakfast, or giggling over a book,' Robbie said. 'She says that's *childish and stupid.*'

The new boy peered at Robbie. 'But your aunt laughs,' he said. 'I hear her laughing most evenings.'

'She laughs at the TV,' said Brenda. 'But only at the nasty things, like the washed-up dirty-mouthed comedians.'

'Anyway,' said the boy, 'the librarian heard me laughing. She told me to come in *at once*, so of course I did. I went inside... and she said *What's your name?* so I said Tom... she said *Come here!* and I did, and then *Closer!* so I did... and then **Closer!!!** so I did and then... well, here I am.'

'Poor child,' said Grandma.

Tom peered at her. 'You sound like my grandma,' he said. 'I like her. She never makes me nervous.'

'Do you get nervous a lot, dear?' asked Grandma.

'All the time. About everything. I worry about school, then about the school holidays. I worry about getting sunburnt, and I worry about the darkness. I worry *a lot* about the darkness, especially when Bad Santa's there with his smelly elves and scary teddy bears that have evil eyes and the reindeer that try to eat you!'

'You're weird,' said Brenda. 'But I think I like you.'

'Me, too. The skinny ones are the tastiest!' said Wolfie.

Tom gasped again.

'Joke!' growled Wolfie. 'I gave up eating boys yesterday.'

Tom didn't looked convinced. 'If you're hungry,' he said, 'I've got a little kitchen I can make hot chocolate in. You'll have to watch out for the slugs though…'

They had a cup of hot chocolate each, and only Tom found a slug in his. However… Brenda had a caterpillar, Robbie had a worm, Grandma nearly swallowed a beetle and Wolfie found a small mouse swimming in his.

As they sipped their drinks carefully, they worked out what had happened.

'The books must be linked,' said Brenda.

'A *series* of books,' said Grandma.

'But that's backward,' Tom reasoned. 'Red Riding Hood's story should be after mine. *I* was the here before Red!'

This is a scribbly hat by Ara, with help!

'It's the way they're lined up on the shelf, I think,' said Robbie. 'Red's is the last on the right. That means the end of her book faces the beginning of yours. So we went straight from one story to the other.'

'Let's go back,' said Brenda. 'Erase *"The End"* and put us back in our own book. Then we'll look for another way out.'

'What?' asked Tom, alarmed, rising from his seat. 'Go back? And leave me here?'

His face had gone pale. He said in a voice that quavered, 'I can't take any more. It's *horrible*. You *can't* leave me!'

'It *would* be unkind to go back,' said Grandma.

'So – we'll have to go forward?' asked Robbie. 'To the end of Tom's story?'

'Or do you mean all the way to the very end?' Wolfie growled. 'Through all the books?'

'Of course,' Grandma said, taking out her knitting. 'That way, we can save all the children trapped in them.'

'No!' shouted Brenda. 'Going forward will take *ages*. If we rewrite Tom's story, we'll go through to the next book, won't we? That's the book the witch is going read on Sunday. *She'll find out!* So if we go forward, we'll have to wait a whole week before we can do each story!'

'Oh,' said Robbie. 'And there are eight books in total.'

'Bother!' said Tom.

'Howlllll!' said Wolfie.

'Unless –', said Grandma, 'Unless we can get through one story a day, and two on the last day. That way, we would finish the whole series before the witch tries to read the next book and finds that it's been changed.'

'Brilliant!' said everyone at once - except for Robbie, who looked worried. He said:

'Okay. I'll try. But you'll all have to help with ideas.'

Tom said timidly, 'Could we start *now*? You see, it's almost midnight and Bad Santa usually comes down the chimney just about now. Last night, he was a headless monster covered in blood...'

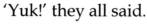

'Yuk!' they all said.

'I'll do my best,' said Robbie, taking out the black book and the strange pen.

Bad Santa and the King

The voices

The King sounds bossy. If he wants a teddy, he expects you to give it to him *now*, without any argument. And since he knows that anything he says is always perfect, he pronounces every word carefully, in rather a rich accent.

Bad Santa sounds like a pirate. **Arrrrr!** The more you exaggerate his accent, the better it will sound, matey. Just imagine you're making your least favourite teacher walk the plank. *Har har!*

His Reindeer don't say anything, but snort and neigh in a wild, piratey fashion. They also chuckle evilly to themselves as they give sneaky kicks and nips to anyone who walks past.

The Bunnies have tough bunny voices, shouting "Peace and Happiness!" like a squad of American Marines. However, they're laid back and ultra-cool. Nothing bothers them; *nothing* – except people who can't count. (And if you want to know more about the bunnies, and why they insist there are seven of them, you'll need to read Wicked Tales One and Wicked Tales Two).

Santa's voice is jolly and plump and chock full of goodness & light. You'd think that nothing unhappy had ever happened to him... but when he talks about his old sleigh and his reindeer, there's a sad sigh in his voice.

The Children in Santa's grotto are loud, rude and a little crazy. Just like most of your class, in fact.

The story

Long ago – before most things had been invented - there was a young Prince who was rich and selfish and spoiled and *very* annoyed with his Christmas presents. He had a carriage with two fine ponies, a football covered in gold velvet, a box of chocolates the size of your bed and a fish tank full of sharks. But he still felt he hadn't been given the presents he deserved.

On the day after Christmas, he was walking about the city in a bad mood when he saw a boy his own age – but thin and pale and dressed in rags - carrying a small, brown teddy bear.

There was something wonderful about the teddy's eyes: they were so warm and kind. The Prince wanted that teddy and immediately sent a squad of soldiers to take it. But the poor boy, weak though he seemed, dodged into a maze of alleyways and disappeared.

The Prince had posters placed on every street corner of the city, offering a reward for the teddy. No one replied.

Then he had all the shopkeepers and toymakers dragged

into the palace, where he questioned them about the teddy he had seen. But they all listened to his description, shook their heads and said:

'Your Majesty, this is like no bear made by man. The colour – the shape – the size – the kind eyes and gently smiling mouth: all those things mean that this is one of Santa's own teddies, made by his elves.'

The Prince raged at them, shouting and stamping his feet. 'Santa doesn't exist! He's just a story! Presents are given to us by our parents and friends and grateful subjects!'

The toymakers and shopkeepers all said apologetically, 'Yes, your Majesty. Most presents do come from friends and family. But Santa also makes some for children who will otherwise get no presents. Also, he brings some for the children who have been especially good.'

'Ha!' said the Prince. 'That can't be true, because *I* didn't get a present from Santa, and *I'm* the most important child in the kingdom!'

They didn't reply, because there's not much you can say to people who think they're Very Important – and also because they didn't want to have their heads cut off.

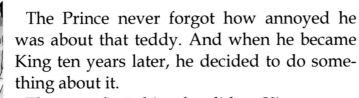

The Prince never forgot how annoyed he was about that teddy. And when he became King ten years later, he decided to do something about it.

The very first thing he did as King was to make a new law: no one was allowed to have a teddy bear. All teddies were to be surrendered at the Palace.

Thousands of teddies were handed in by weeping children, and the King studied each teddy and each child who brought it. None of the teddies given up was the right one, and they were all thrown onto the Royal Bonfire.

Now the King was *furious*. He sent soldiers to search all the houses. They found three teddies that hadn't been handed in: and three families were put in prison. But still the right teddy hadn't been found.

The King sulked and brooded for the rest of the year. Christmas approached and the King drove his carriage around the city streets, scowling at the happy children and shaking his fist at the bright windows of the toy shops.

Bad Santa

Then one night, a mysterious hooded figure in a black robe trimmed with red fur came to the palace. He said, 'I've heard the King wants one of Santa's toys. If that's true, he can meet me in the Royal Gardens at midnight.'

When the King arrived, a man stepped out from the shadows and pulled back his hood. His face was old, sly and scarred. He had a big gold ring in one ear, a black patch over one eye, long dirty hair and a red and black bandana tied about his head. He looked like a pirate.

'They calls me **Bad Santa**!' said the man (he sounded like a pirate, too). 'Santa says Ho ho ho; I says **Yo** ho ho! Anything Santa can do, I can undo. What he makes, I breaks. What he gives, I takes. Like this!'

He waved an arm in the air. At the end of his dirty black jacket cuff was not a hand, but a hook. And impaled on the hook was a toy Santa.

The King said dismissively, 'One toy on a hook doesn't prove anything at all!'

'Ha!' said Bad Santa. 'Look here, then!'

He whistled, and two evil-looking reindeer wearing black eye patches emerged from the shadows, pulling a wooden sleigh shaped like a pirate ship. The sleigh was piled high with toys and flew a skull and crossbones from a flagpole.

'Santa thinks he's so clever!' hissed Bad Santa. 'He thinks he's so *good*! But - arrrr - I can outsmart him, any day of the year. Well – *almost* any day...'

'Almost?' asked the King.

'Christmas Day, he gets the better of me,' Bad Santa said bitterly. 'But that's all! It takes me three hundred and sixty four days to undo what he does on one day: *but I does it!* My pirate sleigh and my pirate crew and my evil reindeer: we thieve and plunder without pause, crisscrossin' round and round the earth so that daylight never falls upon us.'

'But *why?*' asked the King.

''Cause I *hates* him!' shouted Bad Santa. 'I hates his silly laugh and his pretty toys and his cute elves. I hates his red cloak and pointed boots! I hates him 'cause he gets all the attention and I gets none! Just like when we was children!'

'What?' asked the King. 'You mean –'

'Yes! I hates him 'cause he's my twin brother! *I* could have been Santa, *I* could have been the one they all talks about and the kids all love. But he wouldn't let me. He **stole** my chance to be famous!'

'Oh,' said the King. 'So he's as bad as you are?'

'Nah! He's good and jolly - *and I hates him for it!* When we was kids, he was always the favourite. And the nicer he

was, the kinder our parents treated him. I was jealous of
that, so I became nasty and spiteful - and the worse I was,
the worse they treated me. And day by day, he became
nicer, I became meaner, and they became
more and more unfair until - '

Bad Santa stopped and said softly, *'But I'll
tell you that story another day...'*

The King said, 'I see. Your brother took
your big chance to be famous... so now you
take his toys. Including his teddies? His special teddies?'

'Aye,' said Bad Santa, winking his one eye.
'I takes 'em all! Ho ho ho – yo ho ho - *yar har harrrrrr!'*

'Good!' said the King. 'Would you have a special teddy
with you? If it's the right one, I'll buy it.'

'Arrrr.....' said Bad Santa thoughtfully and slyly. 'They's a
bit tricky to find, them special teddies. That would cost you
a lot of money…'

The King said, 'I don't see why a teddy should be harder
to come by than any other toy.'

'Arrr, well... I used to waste a lot of valuable time tryin' to
nick my brother's special toys. My crew and I used to sneak
into children's rooms and take the toys from their very
arms. Har har! You should've heard 'em wail! But it's much
easier to take *ordinary* toys from the ungrateful little brats
that doesn't love 'em. Give 'em five toys and they've broken
one before lunch and have lost the others under the couch.
Besides – well - there's a story about special teddies, you
know? *But I'll tell you that story another day...'*

'Have - you - **got** - one??!' the King shouted.

Bad Santa shook his head. 'I sold the last one yesterday.
And a cute little teddy it was, too: with that sweet smile and
that kind look in its little teddy eyes. Soft and brown and
fluffy all over, with ears that –'

'Enough!' shouted the King. 'I don't want a teddy recipe, I
want a teddy! Get me one!'

Bad Santa looked even more sly than usual. 'Arrrr,' he said. 'Maybe we can find a way to get one, if we works together. You helps me, I helps you....'

'Why should I help a villain like you?' asked the King. 'I'm a King, not a dirty pirate!'

''Cause you're a man after me own heart! When I'd heard there was a king takin' teddies from children, I thought to meself, *"Bad Santa, there's a man with a soul as dark and devious as your own. A man with a heart as cold as an iceberg! **He'll** help you!"* And I'm right, aren't I?'

The King was not at all pleased with having his heart compared to an iceberg. 'I *might* help you,' he said stiffly, 'but *only* if you can get me one of those special teddies.'

'I can get you one at Christmas,' Bad Santa promised, 'but only if you follow my evil plan. Lean close, and I'll whisper it to you....'

Bunnies with guns

He whispered long and low, and the King nodded

until Bad Santa said, 'Lastly, we needs a gun. A *big* gun.'

'But that's impossible!' the King insisted. Guns haven't been invented yet!'

Bad Santa turned and pointed with his hook towards the sleigh. Five ragged pirates stood up in it, wearing pirate hats or headscarves, and with big gold pirate-type rings in their ears... their long, long, furry ears.

The King said in a puzzled whisper, 'But they've got bunny ears!'

'Arr, that's so. That's because they're *bunnies*.'

'Bunny pirates?' the King asked. 'How amusing!'

'I wouldn't laugh if I was you!' whispered Bad Santa. 'And whatever you do, *don't* count them!'

The Bunnies were now pointing five long, shiny things at the King.

'Oh... so those are *guns*, I assume,' said the King. 'But why would bunnies have weapons? '

Bad Santa answered, 'Cos they ain't just any old bunnies. They's *Easter* Bunnies!'

'Yeah,' called a deep bunny voice from the group standing in the sleigh. 'We're the Seven Easter Bunnies!'

'Yeah! The Seven Easter Bunnies!' the others chorused.

'And though we have guns, we only use them in non-violent vegetarian ways for peaceful purposes!'

'Yeah! Peace and Happiness!'

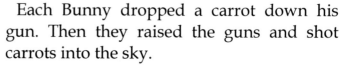

Each Bunny dropped a carrot down his gun. Then they raised the guns and shot carrots into the sky.

'Peace and Happiness!' they cried.

About a mile away, an old witch was pro-nouncing the baby princess's doom at her Christening Party. 'When little Beauty is ten years old,' she croaked, 'she will prick her finger on a... on a...'. She looked up into the sky, her mouth open in surprise. '... a carrot???' she asked won-deringly as an orange pointy vegetable dropped towards her and then made a hole in her black hat... and in her head.

Half a mile away, the King's Horses were piecing together a huge egg named Humpty Dumpty. 'Hey guys!' neighed one. 'We've almost done it! One piece to go! Dobbin, you put it in. Bit of glue.... There – look – he's good as new now!' The horses all stood back to admire the perfectly shaped egg. Just then something dropped from the sky. A moment later, the horses were covered in gooey egg white, egg yolk and bits of eggshell.

*A quarter of a mile away, the Big Billy Goat Gruff was lowering his head and pointing his big horns at the Troll. 'No, Mister Troll,' he bleated gruffly. 'I am going to eat **you** up!' He ran for-ward, snorting triumphantly... a carrot shaped missile fell from the sky... he fell down dead, with a carrot-sized hole in him. 'Dat's nice,' said the Troll, picking him up. 'Kebabs for dinner!'*

Right overhead, a flock of geese were honking happily as they flew away for their summer holiday…

Two dead geese fell at the feet of the Bunnies.

'Odd,' said one Bunny. 'They keep doing that...'

'Seven?' asked the King. 'But there's only five of you!'

The Bunnies calmly reloaded their guns, this time with round things that looked like chocolate Easter eggs.

'We're gonna pretend we didn't hear that,' said one Bunny, pointing his gun at the King.

'Yeah, because we're *peaceful* bunnies.'

The King counted them again. 'But there *are* only five of you!' he insisted.

All the Bunnies were pointing their guns at him now.

'We don't like people who can't count...'

'... They oughta be shot...'

'... So maybe you're gonna say you're sorry.'

'No!' said the King. 'I'm the King of this country, and I don't have to say I'm sorry, *ever*!'

'He said "sorry",' said one Bunny, pointing his gun away.

'I didn't!' insisted the King.

'Hey - we heard you say it. You can't take it back now.'

The King stamped his foot. 'I used the *word* "sorry". I didn't *say* that I was sorry! I'm *not* sorry!'

'You just said it three more times,' said another Bunny, pointing his gun away, too. 'You must really be sorry.'

The King shouted, 'I'm *not* sorry! Not! *Not!* **Not!**'

'He said it again,' a third Bunny said. 'I never met a man so sorry for being unable to count.'

'I *can* count!' roared the King. 'And there's only five of you! *Not* seven!'

Five guns were pointing at him again.

'Apologise!' shouted five voices.

'Won't!'

Bang! One trigger was pulled and the King was knocked flying. When he opened his eyes, he was lying flat on his back, covered in melted chocolate.

'This tastes *really* good,' he said, licking chocolate from his fingers as he got to his feet. 'But there's still only five of –'

Bang! He was lying on his back again, covered in chocolate ice cream this time.

'Look,' he said, standing up again and licking ice cream from his collar. 'You can't do this. I'm the King! And if *I* say there's only five –'

Bang! This time he had a green, slippery mess all over his chest and face - and sticking his hair together.

He tasted it. 'Spinach!' he said. 'But why is it so slimy and sticky?'

One Bunny looked embarrassed. 'I'm allergic to spinach,' he said. 'I sneezed in it.'

'Me too,' said another.

'I think we all did...' said a third.

'Oh *yuk!*' said the King. He took out a large white handkerchief and wiped his face with it.

'He's surrendering!' said a Bunny.

'Yeah! The white flag!'

'We accept your surrender and your apology.'

'I *didn't* surrender!' shouted the King. 'And I didn't apologise!' He shook his fist at them.

One Bunny said to the others, 'There – he said ***surrender*** and ***apologise.*** And he's waving that white flag at us again.'

'What a nice guy,' said another.

'No!' shouted the King. 'I didn't! I'm not! *And there's only five of you!*'

'Oh dear,' said the head Bunny with a sigh. 'Now we're gonna have to get tough. Which is difficult, because we're gentle bunnies who love peace and happiness.'

'Peace and happiness!' shouted the others, and one Bunny shot his gun into the air again.

There was a surprised *honk* and another goose fell at their furry feet.

'Now look what you've done,' said the head Bunny. 'That's

what happens when people can't count!'

He raised his gun and pulled the trigger.

Bang! The King got up from the ground again, slowly. He poked at the brown, smelly mess that had splattered him from head to foot. He licked his finger and was immediately sorry he'd done so. 'What's this?' he spluttered.

'Cow Pat Surprise,' said the Bunny. 'Want another? We've got a special offer on them today. Five for the price of seven!'

'Hold on.' One Bunny put his gun down and pulled out a calculator. He poked its buttons for a while.

'That's wrong,' he said finally.

'You mean it's the other way around - seven for the price of five?' asked the King.

'I'm not sure,' said the Bunny. 'This calculator doesn't have any batteries in it.... They haven't been invented yet.'

The first Bunny said to the King, 'You said "seven" about a minute ago.'

'Yes,' said the King. 'I did.'

'That's all right, then,' said the Bunny. 'We accept your apology and your admission that there are seven of us.'

'I –' began the King. But when he saw the Bunnies reaching for their guns again, he said hastily, 'I agree. *Seven*. A good number, that. One of my favourites.'

The next day, the King went to the Royal Armoury, where all the swords and arrows and spears are made.

'I want a gun,' he said. 'A *big* gun. A gun that can shoot down a flying reindeer.'

'But your Majesty – guns haven't been invented yet!'

'I brought a drawing of one for you. It – it's got some splashes of cow pat on it. Sorry about that....'

As the royal armourers set about making a Reindeer Gun, the King declared a new law: teddy bears were to be allowed again, but only in the royal city, and only from Christmas Day onwards.

'That'll do it!' Bad Santa had whispered in the King's ear.

'Hundreds of children will ask Santa for a teddy bear this Christmas! Har har!'

'So we'll shoot down the sleigh and take all the teddies!' said the King. 'But what if we miss?'

'Arrrrr, we can cover that. All we needs to do is find out where the children live... And that's gonna be easy!' And Bad Santa laughed: an evil, scheming pirate laugh.

Santa's grotto

Soon afterwards, Santa's grotto was set up inside the castle. Santa looked surprisingly like the King, but the children knew he must be the real Santa because he said *Ho ho ho*, had a big white beard and a big tummy, and was surrounded by a group of tall Elves armed with big swords and spears. And besides, all the other Santas had mysteriously disappeared from the city...

One by one, children were led forward by an Elf in armour and lifted onto Santa's bony knee. Another Elf stood at Santa's side, writing names and addresses and presents in a large red book.

It started badly....

'Ho ho ho. What do you want for Christmas, little boy?'

'I'm a girl.'

'Oh. Well, you're a very UGLY girl. You can have face paints to make you look better. Take her away!'

'Waaaaaa!'

'Ho ho ho. Do you want a teddy, little boy?'

'Is it a special teddy?'

'Yes.'

'Does it have an extra leg?'

'No.'

'Does it have just one eye, and the eye shoots out a laser beam and melts dollies?'

'No. Lasers haven't been invented yet.'

'Does it have a big saw on one arm that it uses to rip other toys to pieces?'

'No. It has a happy smile.'

'That's boring. I don't want a boring teddy.'

'How'd you like a smack on the head instead? Because that's all you're getting from Santa this year!'

(Whack!)

'Waaaaaa! Oh... I just wet myself....'

'Take him away!'

'Ho ho ho. Hello, little girl. What would you like –'

'You smell of wee! Have you wet yourself, Santa?'

'No, it wasn't me. It was the little boy –'

'Your knee's all wet! Waaaaa! Santa's covered in wee!'

'Take her away!'

After changing his Santa outfit, the King tried again.

'Ho ho ho. What do you want for Christmas, my child?'

'I want a book to read.'

'And a teddy?'

'No, just a book.'

'That's a *stupid* present. Get lost, kid.'

'Do I get a book? One I can read all by myself?'

'Yeah, yeah. Write it down, Guard – I mean, Elf. One book he can read by himself. Take him away!'

'Hooray!'

'The kid's crazy! Why's he so happy about a book?'

'Ho ho ho. What do you want for Christmas, little girl?'

'I want a cooking pot.'

'Why?'

'So my mother can cook nice food in it.'

'Okay. Good present. Anything else?'

'Can it be a magic cooking pot that fills itself every time you empty it?'

'No. But I can put a special teddy in it.'

'That's weird. Who would want to cook a teddy?'

'The teddy is for playing with, dimwit girl.'

'But I don't feel like playing when I'm hungry all the time, dimwit Santa.'

'All right! One cooking pot, plus a few potatoes to go in it. And a teddy?'

'Deal!'

'Take her away....'

'Ho ho ho. What do *you* want for Christmas, funny look-ing boy?'

'I want to be with my family.'

'And I expect you'd like a teddy too?'

'No. The other thing I want is for the King to be punished.'

'Ho ho – What??! That's a *stupid* present. *No one* wants to hurt the wonderful King.'

'I do. He put all my family into prison. He's a BAD King.'

'You don't understand, kid. Royal people are never *bad*.

We – I mean *they* - they can do whatever they like. They make the rules, okay?'

'No! I want the King to suffer **big time**.'

'Look, you creepy little boy: you can have *one* of your two wishes. Good old Santa will make sure that you get to be with your family at Christmas. Isn't that great?'

'Yay!' the boy exclaimed.

'Guard!' the King ordered. 'I mean, *Elf!* Take this boy to his family!' Then he whispered into the Elf's ear, 'And then *leave* him in prison with them!'

'*Thank you!*' said the excited, happy boy.

'Yo ho ho! I mean – *Ho* ho ho!' said the King. He was very annoyed with being called a bad king, so he pushed the child off his knee, roughly. But when he did this, he also granted the boy's other wish because the boy landed on the King's right royal foot and crunched his royal big toe.

'*Owwww!*' the King exclaimed. 'Take him away!'

'Yes sir!' shouted the Elf, saluting and banging his spear on the ground – well, almost on the ground because the King's big toe was in the way and got crunched again.

'Yiiiiiii!'

Interruption

The story had to stop at this point because they heard Robbie's aunt shouting for him.

'Robert!' she called again, more sharply this time. 'I know you can hear me!'

Robbie wasn't going to answer. But then his aunt came to the bookshelf and reached for the Red Riding Hood book.

Brenda pinched Robbie hard and he yelped. His aunt's

hand paused, her fingers touching the black leather.

'Owwww!' Robbie said. 'Aunt Mildred, please let me out! Red is being horrid to me! And – '

Wolfie snarled. Robbie added:

'And the wolf! Please save me from the wolf!'

Aunt Mildred's low, dry laugh echoed through the eight books on the shelf. 'I'll *never* let you out!' she promised. 'You'll be in there forever and ever, each day worse than the one before. You're a noise and a nuisance and an interfering little brat - just like your mother was. Which reminds me: I came to tell you that your father phoned today. I told him you've had a bad report from school, you kicked next door's dog, and you broke one of my favourite china dolls. Ha! And by the way – your mother's worse. *Much* worse.'

Robbie said, 'I hope that's not true.'

'*Hope?!!*' shouted his aunt. That's something I hate about you children – the way you're always hopeful. You've nothing to be hopeful *about*! Your mother *won't* get better.'

Robbie said stubbornly, 'She says...'

'I *know* what she says! She says that good can come out of hard times, even out of her illness. She's a *fool*! Nothing good will come out of it – except that maybe I'll get some of her money when she dies!'

Brenda pinched Robbie again and mouthed at him: *Cry!*

So Robbie made little sobbing sounds. He didn't have to pretend much: he was very near to crying anyway.

The witch moved away, chuckling to herself. They all held their breath until they heard the bedroom door shut. Then Robbie wiped his face and took up his pen again.

'Do you need a rest?' asked Grandma kindly.

'No,' Robbie said. 'I'm okay. Let's finish the story.'

Bad Santa Part Two

Soon the King had a long list of children and their desired presents. Only five wanted a teddy and the King had their addresses: but of course the King wasn't going to wait around for his present. He was going to collect it *before* the children got their grubby hands near it.

On Christmas Eve, the King was sitting on the roof of the palace, scanning the empty skies that darkened as the sun sank into the distant mountains. Beside him was his Reindeer Gun; in the shadows lurked Bad Santa, laughing to himself in a piratical fashion.

The King could hear people singing in the streets below, church bells ringing, laughter and fun. But he ignored all that and stared into the darkness above him.

He jumped up. Something had moved across the dark sky, blotting out the stars. He strained his eyes, following the shadow as it swung from right to left. He sighted along the gun, following the target, and pulled the trigger.

He expected to hear the cry of a wounded animal. But what floated down from the sky was a deep laugh: a big laugh; a laugh from a big and merry heart.

The dark shadow dropped like a stone towards the palace roof, making the King jump to one side. But the shadow stopped a few metres above the roof, then settled gently upon it: a sleek silver sleigh on curved runners.

'Ow!' shouted the King, because the sleigh had landed on his injured toe.

A big man stepped out of the sleigh and laughed. 'You put a hole in my sleigh!' he boomed at the King, still laughing. 'Worse than that, you put a bullet in my bum!'

The big man laughed again, as if being shot in the rear was the funniest thing imaginable.

'We don't say "bum" in the Palace,' said the King stiffly. 'It's rude.'

'All right then,' said Santa – the real Santa. 'You got me in the B-T-M! Ho ho ho!'

The King aimed the Reindeer Gun at Santa. 'Give me the toys!' he ordered.

Santa pointed to the sleigh. 'Help yourself, King.'

The King looked in the sleigh. 'But it's empty!' he shouted. 'It *can't* be empty!'

'Of course it's empty,' said Santa. 'How could I get a billion toys in the back seat of a sleigh? It would weigh a million tons! *And* the toys would get wet when it snows! Besides - just think how long it would take to pack it, and then find the right toy at each house!'

'I *knew* it!' shouted the King. 'You don't give out toys! It's all a myth!'

'Myth?!!' roared Santa. 'The toys are as real as I am! But I've moved with the times. This is a Techno Sleigh, with a real-time uplink to the toy storage drive in hyperspace. Look!' He pressed a button on the sleigh's dashboard and a screen lit up. *Palace Central* it read. *Children 8 - Presents 7.'*

He poked at the screen again. Seven parcels appeared in the back seat of the sleigh.

Santa said, 'I could have sent the presents directly to their rooms. But I thought you'd like to see how it's done.'

The King's eyes had lit up when the presents appeared; and when he spoke, he sounded like a little boy again: 'Is one of those presents for me?' he asked hopefully.

'Ho ho ho – don't make me laugh, King!' said Santa. 'You haven't been good since... *(he typed on the screen again)*... since you were three. And *that* was mostly luck! No, these are for the servants' children.'

The King asked, 'Only one present each? And one of them doesn't get anything? That's not fair!'

'Parents buy most of the toys,' said Santa. 'I can't get round to everyone. But in many houses there's a present that no one knows where it came from.'

'But it's your job to look after everyone!' said the King.

'No,' said Santa. 'It's *your* job! If you people were generous enough, I wouldn't have to go round all the poor houses and poor countries that you don't care about.'

'It's not *my* fault,' said the King. He pointed at the presents and asked, 'Are there any teddies in those parcels?'

Santa pressed another button and looked at a list on the screen. 'No.'

'I want a teddy!' the King shouted. 'Get me one now!'

Santa shook his head. 'Doesn't happen like that. Presents are delivered to match the space-time overlap.'

'What?'

'The only time I can call up a present is when we're at the house where the child lives. That makes sure I give the right present to the right child.'

'Then take me to a house with a special teddy!' the King commanded. 'I have a list here.'

'Is it the same as mine?' asked Santa. He tapped on the keyboard and compared the screen with the King's list.

He said, 'Let's look at the first on the list... Little boy...

wants his family let out of prison. Ooooh, *naughty* King! You shouldn't have put them in prison in the first place!'

The King said stiffly, 'I'm the KING. *I* can do whatever *I* want. You can't say *"shouldn't"* to me!'

Santa looked at him. 'You're just like my brother!' he exclaimed. 'You don't know the difference between *could* and *should*! Nor did he! Ho ho ho!'

'What? Could and should?'

Santa took something out of the glove compartment of the sleigh. 'I'll show you!' he said. 'Look at this hammer, ho ho! Now, your Majesty, I *should* use this hammer to bash in nails, right? But I *could* use it on the wrong sort of nails - *toe*nails!'

Santa bashed the King's bad toe with the hammer.

'Owwwww!' shouted the King. 'You shouldn't do that!'

'Ho ho ho!' Santa laughed. 'You're learning, King! But actually, in this case I *should* do it, because that's what's written on the list: *"Make the King suffer!"* Like this!'

He brought down the hammer with another *thump.* 'You see, King *(Thump!)*, you're no more important than anyone else. And no less important. Merry Christmas! *(Thump!)'*

Santa studied the list again while the King hopped about clutching his foot. 'That's half the boy's wishes done, anyway. You can let him out of prison later tonight.'

'*Owwww!* I won't!' said the King. '*Owwowwowwwow!*'

'Ho ho ho... I bet you *will!*' Santa raised the hammer.

'Okay,' the King said sulkily.

Santa said, 'That's settled, then. I'll be on my way.' He climbed back onto the sleigh and sat down. But he jumped up again immediately.

'Ow!' he exclaimed. 'My BTM *really* hurts!'

'Ha!' said the King. 'Serves you right!'

Santa said, 'But I won't be able to drive the sleigh!'

A voice spoke from the shadows:
'*I'll* do it!'

Bad Santa stepped forward. 'Remember *me*?' he asked.

Santa peered at him through the darkness. 'Daddy!' he exclaimed.

'No!'

'Oh,' said Santa. 'Mummy? Why are you wearing that eyepatch, Mummy?'

'*That's a long story,*' said Bad Santa. 'And I ain't Mummy. Look at this scar on my arm! And the one on my cheekbone! And the tattoo on my leg! Do you recognise me *now*?'

'Grandma?' asked Santa.

'*No!* Look at me: you and I grew up together! We played and fought and laughed and cried together!'

'Poopy my pet parrot?' asked Santa. 'Is that really you? How changed you are, Poopy!'

'No!' cried Bad Santa – and he kicked Santa in the backside, hard.

'Ow!' said Santa. 'I recognise *that!* You must be my twin brother! Ho ho ho! *Ouch ouch ouch!*'

'Aye, I'm your brother. Did you miss me?'

'No!' said Santa, rubbing his backside.

'I didn't miss you, either. But it's good to see you again, 'cause it's *payback time*! I'm gonna take your new, pretty sleigh, just like I took your old one!'

'YOU?' roared Santa. '*YOU* were the one who stole my sleigh? And the reindeer... what happened to the reindeer?'

'Har harrrr! Reindeer stew, *that's* what happened!'

Santa gasped. 'You ate them? Rudolf and Prancer and Dancer and Donder and Blitzen and all the others?'

'Not *all* of 'em. Look over there!'

The two reindeer emerged from the shadows, pulling the rickety wooden sleigh.

'Dancer!' exclaimed Santa. 'Prancer!'

Bad Santa laughed. 'And they's all that's left, harrrrr!'

'You really ate Rudolf?' asked Santa sadly.

'I ate old Bignose *first!* Har har!'

Santa went forward and tried to pet the reindeer. But the first one bit his hand and the second bit his... BTM.

'Ouch! Oh, *double* ouch!'

'Arrrr, they still ain't forgiven you for makin' such a fuss over Rudolf, just because he had a shiny nose!'

'Surely not!' said Santa. 'I loved *all* my reindeer - just... just in different ways!'

Dancer and Prancer looked at each other and laughed: long, sneering pirate reindeer laughs.

Santa turned away sadly. As he walked back to the King, Prancer gave him a sneaky kick in the rear.

'*Ouch!* ... Maybe you're right,' said Santa to his brother, regretfully. 'Maybe I shouldn't have had a favourite reindeer. That was wrong.'

Bad Santa kicked his brother in the backside again. 'You never said a truer word. *Never* have favourites! Our parents had a favourite son, and see what happened!'

'Ouch,' said Santa. 'Ouch... ouch... ouch...!'

'Aye. And now it's time to take my revenge. Har harrr!'

'Wait: I'll swap you,' said Santa. 'Take the new sleigh and presents. I'll take the old one and retire. Maybe I can persuade Prancer and Dancer that I'm not totally bad. Maybe, in our old age, we'll find peace and happiness.'

'Peace and happiness!' shouted some voices from the darkness, and five guns were blasted into the air.

Twenty miles away, the evil scientist Goldenbum was gloating over secret agent 007. 'Now, Mister Bond,' he hissed. 'I have tied you securely to this rocket. You have no weapons and no friends. In a few seconds I will press this big red button and you will fly *into the air. You will explode over London and your tiny, tiny pieces will shower down upon your fellow citizens. Ha ha!' ...Bond did not reply. He wiggled his right big toe in a special fashion and a bullet shot from his shoe. The evil scientist fell dead. Bond laughed. 'I am soooo clever!' he said to himself. 'I am the greatest and the best! No one can defeat **me**! Ha ha!' Just then a ball of chocolate ice cream fell from the sky and landed smack in the middle of the big red button. The rocket engine roared and 007 was lifted into space...*

... Zorro leapt further up the hillside. His sword slashed left, right; two more of his assailants fell. Only three left now. 'Ha ha!' he cried. 'So you thought you could overcome the great Zorro! Prepare to die!' He threw his sword spinning in the air from his right hand to his left, caught it and laughed again. 'See! I am the great Zorro! I can do circus tricks in the middle of a battle! Ha ha!' He threw it once more, from left to right this time, then pointed it down at the three attackers. They laughed up at him. He looked down at his hand, puzzled. Instead of a sword, he was holding a carrot. 'Uh oh...' he said.

... Three ducks fell from the sky, landing at Santa's feet.

'At least it makes a change from geese,' said a Bunny.

Santa stared at the Bunnies. 'Is this your pirate crew?' he asked his brother. 'Five *bunnies*? Ho -'

Five guns appeared, pointing at his big, red tummy.

One Bunny said, 'If we weren't peaceful bunnies, we would shoot you now. But we're gonna give you a chance, fat boy. Just say you're sorry that you laughed at us, and **really** sorry that you can't count up to seven.'

Santa said, 'I *can* count! And I wasn't laughing, I was just saying *Ho ho ho*. I say that a lot, because I'm Santa Claus.'

'That's all right,' said a Bunny, pointing his gun away. 'Santa doesn't exist, so we don't have to get mad about the things he never really said anyway.'

A third Bunny said, 'Yeah. He's just an imaginary fat guy from a story.' They began putting their guns away.

'What???' Santa exploded. 'Look, I *do* exist!'

One Bunny said to the others, 'Did you hear something just then? Something ho-ho-hoish?'

'No,' they answered.

'I *do* exist! And there's only five of you!' shouted Santa.

'Can't hear a thing,' said one Bunny, putting on some earphones and listening to Bunny Rap music that hadn't been invented yet.

Santa raged, '**You're** the ones who don't exist! There's NO – SUCH – THING – as the Easter Bunny!'

There were five guns pointing at him again. The head Bunny spoke calmly: 'You don't mean that. You're just upset because you're an imaginary character in a story.'

Santa asked, 'But if I'm *imaginary*, why are you pointing those guns at me? *Ho ho ho!*'

'Because we've got good imaginations,' said a Bunny.

'And now we're gonna have to go against all our peaceful principles and shoot you,' said another.

'But that doesn't matter,' said yet another, 'because it's not really going to hurt you, since you don't really exist.'

Five guns spoke at once.

Santa slowly got to his feet. His red Santa outfit was mostly brownish pink now, and there was a disgusting smell in the air.

'What – is *that*??!' he choked out.

'Chocolate with pig raspberry filling,' said a Bunny.

'What – (*yukkkk!*) – what's a pig raspberry?' he groaned.

A Bunny said, 'Ummm... it's the kind of raspberry noise and smell a pig makes when it's eaten too many raspberries.'

Santa threw off his smelly cloak and turned to the King and Bad Santa. 'I'll show you how the sleigh works,' he said. The dashboard lit up, showing a map of the world.

'Wow!' said the King. 'Can we go anywhere?'

'Of course. You choose.'

The King leaned forward and tapped on a bright point. 'Mount Everest,' he said. 'Always wanted to go there.'

The sleigh accelerated away so fast that the King thought he was going to fall out. But a few seconds later they were hovering above a snowy mountain, near to a tiny snow-bound cottage.

Santa was reading the screen. '*Two presents... deliver?* See: you just press this button. Done! Ho ho ho!'

'*Yo* ho ho, you mean!' snarled Bad Santa. 'It's *my* sleigh now! And they're *my* presents, too!'

They sped about the globe delivering presents and finished the evening in the King's own city. Santa let the King take the presents to the door of each house, and the King was astonished when one after another of his subjects threw their arms about him and thanked him for the simplest of things – a doll, a bowl, a new axe.

With every house, the King looked more thoughtful and Bad Santa looked more bothered. Then they came to the house of the girl who had asked for the cooking pot. Santa pressed the button, sighed and shook his head.

'Can't do it,' he said.

'Why not?' asked the King. Has she been bad?'

'No, not at all. She's a great little girl. But I can't give her something as useless as a cooking pot.'

Bad Santa banged his hook on the dashboard. 'Give it to her!' he shouted. 'It's what she wanted! Arrrrrr!'

'I can't do it,' said Santa. 'I can't give her a cooking pot when there's nothing to put in it. They have no food, not even a piece of bread.'

'*I* have food!' the King said. 'She can have some of mine!'

Santa looked at him. 'Okay. That's a deal. Her family get a plateful each of your palace Christmas dinner. And what about the other families with no food?'

'They can have the same!'

'Oooooh,' said Santa, shaking his head. 'That'll mean you won't have much left for yourself. Probably a couple of sprouts and a bowl of soup for Christmas.'

'Do it!' shouted the King recklessly. 'I like soup!'

Next they came to the house of the boy who wanted a book for Christmas.

'No, not this one either,' said Santa.

'He can have one of my books,' said the King.

'Mine, too,' said Bad Santa. 'Got plenty of books in the old sleigh! Books I stole from you, arrrr! Yo ho ho!'

'We've got seven books,' said the Bunnies. 'We could spare two. Just on loan, of course...'

'That's not the problem,' Santa said. 'The boy asked for a book that he could read himself. And he can't read.'

'Why not?' asked Bad Santa. 'Is he a lazy little toad?'

'No. He can't read because there's just one school in this kingdom, and that's only for rich people.'

The King exclaimed, 'I'll build some schools! And pay for good, kind teachers to work in them!'

'Oooooh,' said Santa, shaking his head. 'If you do that, you can't afford gold plates to eat off.'

'Gold is over-rated,' said the King. 'China plates will do.'

... Then they came to the prison. 'Don't say it,' said the King. 'I'll let the families out. All of them.'

'That's not what I was going to say,' said Santa. 'Look at the screen.'

The screen read: *Special teddy. Deliver?*

'Special teddy!' exclaimed the King. 'At last!'

'Arrrr!' exclaimed Bad Santa. 'At last! Give it to me!'

Santa pressed a button. 'You can take this present to the little boy,' he said. He handed the King a wonderful teddy, with a warm smile and shining eyes.

The King looked at the teddy. The teddy smiled back at him. 'He really is special,' the King breathed.

'It's for a special boy,' said Santa. 'Didn't you notice something special about him?'

'He was angry at me,' said the King. 'They mostly are.'

'That wasn't what I meant. He was also very ill. He won't last more than a month.'

'No!' said the King. 'That can't happen! I'll send the Royal Doctor! A team of nurses! The best food possible!'

Santa shook his head. 'That won't help,' he said gently. 'But you could give him the teddy.'

'Why?'

'Do you remember that special teddy you saw, long ago? You couldn't find that teddy afterwards, could you? Well, this is why: these are the most special bears in the world. I only give them to children who are so very ill that they will die soon. That little boy you saw ten years ago wasn't long for this world; and when he passed on, he took the teddy with him.'

'Oh,' said the King.

'So the teddy you have in your hands – you can keep it, or give it to the little boy inside that door. It's up to you.'

'*And* me!' said Bad Santa. 'It's *my* teddy now!'

The King gave the teddy to Bad Santa. Bad Santa looked into its soft teddy eyes, prodded its teddy tummy gently with his hook, and handed it back.

The King looked at the teddy one last time, then went to knock on the door.

A little later, the sleigh settled upon the roof of the palace again, its silver sides twinkling in the starlight.

Bad Santa shouted, 'Har Harrrrr! *I'm* Santa now! And I'm gonna do it *my* way! I'm gonna give presents to BAD children as well as good ones! And I'm gonna nick presents from the rich ones and give 'em to the poor!'

'Good idea,' said Santa. 'I'll take a year off. Maybe ten.'

Bad Santa said to the King, 'I'll be back next year, and you can help me again. Just don't shoot me in the BTM like you did my brother! Ho ho ho! - Sorry, I mean *Yo* ho ho!''

'I won't,' said the King. 'No more shooting. No more pris-

ons. Just peace and happiness...'

'Peach and hoppiness!' shouted one Bunny.
The others looked at him. 'Sorry,' he said.

'Peace and happiness!' they all shouted.

*A large yacht was anchored just off the coast. Three large pigs
and their large wives were lying on the deck, surrounded by piles
of banknotes. They were the only piggy bankers to have escaped
from Red Riding Hood. 'This is the life!' grunted one, swallowing
a plateful of food with one gulp. 'Nothing like it!' snorted another,
pouring a large bottle down its throat. 'We have soooooo much
money!' said a third. 'But we're worth it!'* **'Worth it!'** *they all
chorused. 'Yeah - money's all you need.' They gazed contentedly
at the sky, listening to the sound of the hungry sharks splashing
in the sea. One of the pig wives stuffed banknotes into her mouth
and chewed on them. 'Yeah – money brings you peace and happiness!' she sighed.... Just then, five carrots dropped from the sky
and made five big holes in the boat. It began to sink. The money
began to float away. The waiting sharks turned to one another
and shouted, 'Peace and happiness!'*

Wednesday Afternoon

The sun woke them gently, for its beams were softened and scattered by the leaves of the high trees all about the narrow forest path. They were in a carriage, being pulled along slowly by two bad-tempered reindeer. As the sun climbed directly above them, they came to the edge of the wood. Before them was a broad stream with a wooden bridge across it.

On the other side of the stream was Aunt Mildred's room. The room seemed impossibly big - as if it was a few steps away, even though there was a river in front of it.

The carriage drew to a halt before the bridge and Grandma (who was driving) whispered back to the others:

'Do we go across the bridge?'

'But that's her room! She'll see us!' gasped Tom, who was wearing a new pair of glasses he'd found in the carriage.

'She'll be out,' said Grandma. 'Look - the clock on her wall shows one o'clock.'

'Dinner time!' growled Wolfie, licking his lips.

'Don't *do* that!' said Brenda. 'You made me jump!'

'Sorry,' said Wolfie. 'It's a children's game I used to play. Really fun, too. Gives them a bit of a scare when a real wolf turns up, though...'

'What day is it?' asked Robbie.

Brenda pointed across the river. On Aunt Mildred's wall, by the clock, was a calendar with days crossed through. 'Wednesday,' she said.

'That doesn't mean we have to rush, does it?' asked Wolfie hopefully, licking his lips again.

'No,' said Grandma. 'And I picked up some lovely sausage sandwiches in town.'

'I'll make some tea,' said Tom.

'No you won't!' they all shouted.

They had a picnic on the grass, with the sun spilling over them, and talked about what they wanted to do when they were back in the real world.

'Something different,' said Wolfie. 'I never wanted to be a wolf. When I was a little cub, I kept pretending to be a bird. I even tried jumping off river banks and flapping my paws.'

'Did it work?' asked Brenda, laughing.

'Nah, I just got wet... *What?* You're laughing at me, are you? Look - this is deep and personal. It's *not* funny!'

But everyone was laughing now.

'You once said you wanted to make people laugh,' said Brenda. 'Well, you're doing it now!'

Wolfie sulked. 'I was just a tiny cub,' he grumbled. 'I didn't know any better.'

Grandma smiled at him. 'It's a good story, Wolfie,' she said. 'And you're a natural comic.'

Wolfie shrugged his great, furry shoulders. 'What about *you*, then?' he asked. 'What did *you* want to be when you were little?'

'I always wanted to be a grandma, dear, but I didn't have any children myself. Being caught by the witch has had its good side because now I have lots of grandchildren to look after, and I'm very happy here.'

Brenda asked, 'But where *are* your grandchildren?'

'Oh, I have so many of them now. When a boy is sad and lonely; when a baby is crying in the night; when children need to be brought out of their sulkiness or meanness: at times like those, they need a whispered lullaby or a kind and helpful word.'

Tom looked puzzled. He said, 'But you're stuck in the witch's story! You can't visit anyone!'

Grandma laughed. 'The witch can't watch me all the time, dear, so I often pop out during the evening and do my bit for the children. Of course I can't completely escape, so the children think they've just imagined me. But an imaginary grandma can be very soothing.'

'But – but – but *how*?' asked Brenda.

'I don't know the answer to that, dear,' said Grandma, 'but I do know that the witch can't have it all her own way. The light shines in the darkness, you know.'

'And now we'd better go,' said Robbie. He opened the book and took up his pen. 'How does this sound to you?'

'As the light of a new day grew about them, their carriage rolled through the forest, each turn of the wheels taking them nearer home. The end.'

Goldfish Boy

They drove the carriage to the river and rattled onto the wooden bridge. The reindeer snorted, then flew off into the sky, leaving the carriage rolling by itself.

The bridge took a steep turn downwards and the carriage rolled into the water, sinking quickly. Its wheels went spinning away and its roof lifted off. Its walls dissolved and slid away like brown sugar.

And now they were sitting at the bottom of a deep river. No, not a river: a sea, for the water was salty. And there were some large, scary fish prowling above them...

'I dnt like fiss,' said Tom in an underwater gurgle.

'Wtv you dn??!' shrieked Brenda.

'Iss wt,' said Wolfie. 'And cld!'

'I spect we'll gt used to it,' said Grandma. 'Bt I don't fink I can knit in fiss...'

Robbie looked about him. They were seated on the sandy bottom of a sea that stretched to all horizons. The water surface was far above them. The sun hovered somewhere beyond that, casting a watery light all about.

'Whaff shwee do?' he asked.

'Pardon?' asked Brenda.

Robbie shook his head until his ears cleared. 'What shall

we do?' he tried again.

'Funny, isn't it?' asked Wolfie. 'We're underwater but we can still breathe!'

'Oh no!' exclaimed Tom, who hadn't thought about this until now. He began to cough and choke.

'Drowning!' he groaned. 'Help! Hlp! Hlfffff!'

'You make far too much fuss,' said Brenda. 'You're perfectly all right!'

'Not for long,' said Wolfie, pointing upwards.

The large fish were coming closer. They had a lot of teeth and you could tell that they wanted to use them.

Tom gurgled, 'Drowning *and* eaten by sharks.... Help!'

'Shhh!' Wolfie warned. 'They're coming closer! Look! Oh... the poor goldfish... *he's* a goner, for sure.'

A rather big goldfish was being chased by three sharks. His fins were flapping a zillion times a second, his eyes were rolling, his gills were pumping and his tail was waving weakly. He spiralled down towards the sea bed, with the sharks gliding effortlessly above, taunting him:

'We see ya, fishy!'

'Yeah, you gonna die!'

'Gonna eat ya slow!'

'No, fast!'

'Slow, I'm gonna do it.'

'Den you ain't gonna get any, cos it'll all be gone.'

'Oh. Okay den. Gonna eat ya FAST, fishy!'

The goldfish darted left, right, forward, but always sinking down. His big round eyes cast about for help...

'We ought to help him,' said Robbie.

'No point,' said Wolfie. 'They outnumber us in the tooth department.'

'We still –' Robbie began.

'No way!' said Brenda.

'Ditto!' said Tom, trying to hide behind Grandma.

'What about those others?' asked Grandma, pointing with a knitting needle.

They looked and saw twenty or so small fish hiding within a clump of seaweed, peering up anxiously. The big goldfish was right above them now. He hovered there, looking up at the sharks. Then he darted away.

The sharks hesitated a moment, then swung about in a tight spiral, down and around and down again, and then right down upon the hidden group of worried fish, which they snapped up in seconds.

As the satisfied sharks sped away, Brenda said, 'At least the goldfish got away. *He* was lucky!'

'Lucky?' asked a new voice. 'LUCKY?'

They turned and saw the goldfish himself behind them.

 'Don't you recognise SKILL when you see it?' asked the goldfish. 'And INTELLIGENCE? And PLANNING?'

'Nah,' said Wolfie with a yawn. 'But I *do* recognise a cheat and a liar when I see one.'

The goldfish laughed at this. He said, 'I know you meant that as an insult, but what you're really saying is that I tricked those other fish, and I tricked them *good!* You're right, and I accept the praise and respect you're trying to hide. Glad to meet you. Billy's the name. Billy the Bully.'

'It's *you!*' Tom exclaimed. 'The one in the next book! The one the Witch caught at the goldfish tank!'

'Wait!' ordered Billy, one fin held in the air. 'Get it right! You mean *the one who caught the witch* at the goldfish tank!'

'What??'

'You heard me,' said Billy the Bully Fish. 'There I was at the dentist's, waiting for my mum to come out. There's a tank of goldfish at the end of the room. I'm really, *really* bored, so I go and look at it. I start flicking my finger against the tank, and I can tell you: I scared those fish *silly!*'

'That's not kind,' said Robbie.

Billy looked at him pityingly. 'You're *such* a wimp,' he said. 'I feel sorry for you! Anyway, I was having fun with these fish. Then this bossy woman tells me to stop, because she has a bad tooth and the noise is bothering her. I can see she's a scary lady. But *I'm* not scared.'

'You should have been,' said Brenda. 'She's a witch.'

Billy made a rude sign at her with a fin. '*You're* scared,' he said, 'because *you're* a stupid twerp of a girl. I'm *not!* So I kept on playing with the fish, but hiding it so she couldn't quite see. You should have seen those fish jump! Then I dropped bits of torn up paper into the tank, pretending it was fish food. I bet *that* made them sick when they ate it!'

'That's horrible!' said Tom.

Billy laughed at him. 'You're *pathetic!*' he sneered.

Brenda came to Tom's defence: 'No, he's not!'

 Billy said, 'He's a pathetic little baby, and if he was at *my* school, I would kick him all around the playground! You see: *I'm* tough! So when that old witch made a spell that sucked me into a book she had in her handbag, I *knew* I would get the better of her!'

Wolfie said, 'Yeah, yeah: by becoming a stupid goldfish that gets chased by sharks!'

Billy glared at the wolf. '*Chased?*' he asked. '*Me? I* make the rules around here, fuzzy face!'

Grandma peered at him through her knitting wool, which was floating about like fluffy seaweed. 'You mean that you betrayed the other fish to the sharks?' she asked.

Billy spun about and looked at her. 'Yeah,' he said. 'That's the deal, see. I show the sharks a takeaway dinner, and they leave *me* alone. And soon I'll get in touch with even bigger sharks, and I'll show *them* where the little sharks are. The Witch says if I can do that, I'll have proved how clever and tough I am, and she'll let me be a boy again – *her* boy - and we'll be the best team ever. So you see: she thinks she captured me, but in fact *I* captured *her!*'

Brenda was staring at him with her mouth open. 'But what about your family?' she asked. 'We've come to set you free. You can go home now.'

Billy sneered at her. 'What??' he shouted. 'Go home to *that* bunch of losers? Why should I?'

Tom said, 'Because - because you love them.'

Billy laughed at this.

Grandma suggested, 'Or because *they* love *you*?'

'So?' he replied. 'What do I care about that? What matters to *me* is that they were spoilsports. I couldn't kick the cat or throw mud at the neighbours or spit on my sister. But the Witch isn't like that. *She* understands.'

'She doesn't care about you,' Brenda pointed out.

'So?' asked Billy. 'What does *that* matter? *She* knows I'm special. She's got no kids, and her only nephew is a spineless wimp who's afraid of his own shadow. So *I'm* going to be her *real* family. We're going to make history together. We'll be superstars!'

Tom said quietly, 'That'll never make you happy.'

'Oh, yes it will!' laughed Billy the Bully Fish.

Brenda turned to Robbie and said, 'I've heard enough. Leave Billy behind and let's skip forward to the next book.'

Wolfie growled, 'Some humans are lower than animals. Let's get out of here.'

Robbie looked at Grandma.

'Do the best you can, Robbie,' she said calmly.

Billy the Goldfish rolled onto his back and roared with fishy laughter. 'Hooooo! You weirdos think it matters to me *what* you do! *I* don't care! When I see the Witch, I'm going tell her about this, and then we'll both laugh as she puts you on the fire! Hey – I'm going to shout to her tonight when she's getting ready for bed! I'll make her pick up the book, and she'll find out what you're doing, and *then* you'll be in trouble! Ha! Ha!'

Robbie sighed and took out his pen...

Billy the Bully

The voices

Billy the Bully sounds nasty. An egg boiled for an hour, coated with concrete and then boiled for *another* hour wouldn't be as hard-boiled as Billy. Even when he says nice things, his voice tells you he doesn't really mean them.

The **Crab** says nothing, but his actions speak for him. He's clearly a simple, good-hearted creature who would help anyone, even Billy. He's a bit puzzled by humans because they keep trying to catch him or squash him. This is a pity because he knows the answers to a lot of important questions (such as why birds sing and dolphins play) and would quite like to tell us.

The **Sharks** have low, stupid, chompy voices. Try talking with some food tucked into one cheek – that'll do it, especially if the food is still wriggling and kicking and trying to climb out.

The **Dinner Lady Shark** sounds big and mean. You don't want to mess with her, if you like having more than one foot... or more than no head.

Billy's family sound pleasant and happy. They know they ought to be missing Billy and all his funny little violent ways... but actually, they're quite relieved to have a goldfish instead. *Result!*

The story

Once upon a time there was a bully named Billy. He picked on *everyone*. He pinched his little sister, kicked his little brother and threw stones at the cat. He bit the doctor, said rude words to his teacher and made faces at his grandma. He put pepper on his mum's ice cream, curry powder on the dog's dinner and peanut butter in his dad's beer. He was horrible to everyone he met.

He was walking to school one day, when he decided to go to the beach instead.

Bad idea…

On the beach, you can see the fishermen casting their lines into the water, hoping to catch a fish. What you *can't* see are all the lines that come *out* of the water.

Humans "fish" for fish. Fish also "fish" for humans, though they don't call it that. They call it "peopling".

At the exact moment that Billy said to himself, *'I'll go fishing!'* an enormous young shark named Gutsy (who was on his way to shark school) was saying to himself, *'I'll go peopling!'*

Billy waited until the fishermen weren't looking and snatched a fishing rod from one of their bags. He ran along the beach, looking out to sea.

He saw a dolphin playing near to the beach and threw some rocks at it. The dolphin rose from the water, glared at Billy and swam away.

'Stupid dolphin!' Billy shouted and threw some more

rocks. One of them hit the leg of a seagull that had been swooping over the waves. The gull cawed angrily at Billy and flew off.

'Nah nah! Got you!' Billy taunted it.

Meanwhile, the shark was loading his line and looking towards the beach.

'What shall I catch today?' the shark asked himself. He opened his floating fishing box, which was a very large double clam shell, much bigger that a child. He had a tiny doll for catching little girls, and toy cars for boys. For the adults there were chocolates, packs of gum, cigars, bottles of drink, dresses, fur coats, military medals, high-heeled shoes, bank notes, lottery tickets and promises of riches, popularity, fame and happiness.

As he was poking about in the shell, a small crab swam past. *'That'll do,'* he said, snatching the crab. He tied an invisible line around it and cast it onto the beach.

It landed on the sand near to Billy, who was trying to attach a slug to his hook.

The tiny crab looked up at Billy. Billy looked at the crab.

The crab raised its claws and clicked them at Billy.

'Crab! Squash it!' shouted Billy gleefully.

Billy stamped on the crab. But he missed.

The crab had moved back a few inches. It clicked its claws again and danced left and right.

Billy stamped. Missed. Stamped. Missed again.

The crab kept dancing away and sliding backwards, almost as if someone was reeling it back into the sea (which was true).

Billy dropped his fishing rod and chased the crab. 'I'll get you!' he shouted. 'Stupid crab! I'm going to squash you flat!

I'm going to smash you senseless! I'm going to splat you to smithereens! I'm going to –'

The crab had reached the water now but Billy rushed in after it, stamping and splashing and cursing.

'I'm going to – Mmfff! Grgle! Hlff!'

And within seconds, something had dragged him out to sea.

A dolphin heard Billy screaming for help, and swam up to see what was happening. But when it saw that the screamer was Billy, it shook its head and swam away: because it was the same dolphin he'd thrown stones at.

A seagull swooped down and was just about to snip through the line that the shark was reeling in; but then it saw who was on the end of the line. It swooped up again and hovered over Billy, laughing. Billy felt some gull poo land on his head…

The big shark reeled Billy in and put a net around him. He untied the small crab from the line and dropped it into his clamshell fishing box - to use again another day.

He held the net up with one large flipper. *'What've we got here?'* he asked. *'Ah! A bully! First one I've caught this year! A bit small, though…'*

The shark peered at Billy, upside down in the net. A fist came out of the net and punched him on the nose.

The shark laughed, *'Hey – don't tickle me, small fry!'* He turned the net over and shook Billy out. Several of his shark friends, smelling something tasty, came circling round to see what was happening.

'What'cha got, Gutsy?' called one.

'Bully!' said the shark.

'Give us a bite –' asked another.

'– just a nibble –'

'– bit of a leg –'

'– head maybe? I likes a bit of crunchy…'

Gutsy shook his toothy head. *'Gonna take him home,'* he said. *'Keep him till he's big enough to eat.'*

He poured the water out of his clamshell, dropped Billy into it, and shook it to see if Billy was still alive.

'Funny little fing, ain't he?' asked a shark friend.

'Don't know how they live in all dat air stuff,' said another. *'Dey must feel sick all der time!'*

Billy *was* feeling very sick just now, having first been dragged backwards through the sea, then half drowned, then bounced about in a giant clamshell. He snatched one of the dolls and tried to throw it at the sharks, but it bounced back off the clamshell and hit him.

The sharks roared with laughter.

'Dis is gonna be fun!'

'Can we come to your house and play wiv 'im?'

'I got me a sea scorpion we can put in dere!'

'Turn him upside down!'

'Give 'im something nasty to eat!'

They clustered round, putting their horrid faces to the shell. Billy tried punching them as well, but they just laughed at him.

'Hey, Gutsy – he'll die under der water.'

'Yeah, hoomuns need air.'

Gutsy shut the shell and tucked it under a big fin, saying, *'I'll ask my mum. She'll know what to do.'*

Then the sharks dived steeply, spiralling round and round to the sea bed. Billy's stomach swirled round and round as well. Water began to leak through the rim of the shell. The air inside the shell became thick. It was dark in here and rather smelly.

Gutsy and his friends swam to his cave, where his mum was getting supper ready for later that evening – biting the heads off some fish and throwing them into a big pot (she swallowed the heads).

'Look, Mum!' Gutsy shouted. *'I caught me a bully!'*

'Where'd you get that?' asked Gutsy's mum angrily. *'No – don't tell me – I don't wanna know! But you ain't*

*keepin' it. Take it outside **now** and get rid of it! Then you'd better go to school!'*

'Oh, Mum!' groaned Gutsy. *'He won't cause no trouble, promise! I'll get a tank for him and clean it out every day, and feed him myself. And besides – he'll be a good project for school!'*

Big Mama Shark pried open the clamshell a crack and looked in at Billy. She flashed her teeth at him.

'We ain't got nowhere to keep a boy,' she said to Gutsy. *'You'll have to take it to school. They got a big tank thing in the library for air creatures. But after a month, we're gonna eat it.'*

'Wow, thanks Mum!'

'Off you go to school then. Don't be late again!'

Gutsy and his friends sped away to school. They swam in through the school gates and darted away to their classes – all except for Gutsy, who ran into the one shark he didn't want to meet.

It wasn't the Head Sharkteacher, or Gutsy's own teacher: it was far scarier than that.

It was the Head Dinner Lady. She was a mean old nurse shark, and built like an underwater bus.

She swooped down from behind a rock and Gutsy ran right into her. He bounced off, dropping the clamshell. The shell hit the sea bed and Billy hit his head on the inside of the shell.

Billy heard a loud, heavy shark voice.

'Caught 'cha! Hur hur hur...'

'Uh... sorry, Nursey. I was late fer class and –'

'Speeding in school! Take two squid points! And report to me at lunchtime. You'se gonna be cleaning out the pots! Hur hur hur...'

'Awww, Nursey, c'mon, I wasn't goin' dat fast –'

'And another squid point for arguing! And – what's that smell? It's... it's coming from your school clamshell. You got something nice in there?'

The enormous shark, three metres long and a metre wide, put her hungry mouth against the clamshell and began sucking at it. Billy found himself being pulled towards the widening crack.

Gutsy cried out, *'No – please don't, Nursey! Leave my shell alone!'*

'Hoomun!' she exclaimed. *'I taste hoomun, and you ain't allowed them for lunch. No hoomuns, no sweets, no crisps. Thems the rules!'*

'Haven't got a hoomun!' lied Gutsy. *'Just got me a scuba diver's flipper. Dat's what you're tasting!'*

'Don't believe you!'

'You can have it, Nursey. Here – open wide!'

Gutsy opened the clamshell a little, stuck his fin inside, rummaged around quickly and pulled out an old rubber flipper with a few foot bones still in it. He flung it spinning into the Dinner Lady's wide mouth, so hard that it got stuck in the back of her throat.

'Urgh! Uk! Uk! Uk!' she coughed, sending Gutsy and the

shell spinning across the sea bed. Gutsy snatched up the shell and sped away to class before she could recover.

The clamshell was nearly full of water now. Billy was floating at the top with his nose pressed up into the last tiny bit of stale air. Then Gutsy opened the shell and Billy began breathing in water.

Suddenly Billy was pushed into a large glass tank filled with air. (*You* would take a lid off the top of a tank and drop a goldfish in from above; Gutsy of course had to slide open the lid *underneath* the tank and push Billy *up* into it).

As Billy coughed and spat out the sea water he'd choked upon, he saw a lot of scary shark faces peering in at him. The school was in a huge cave, and it should have been quite dark: but the sharks had collected hundreds of lantern fish and angler fish, and put them in cages all about.

Then a bigger face pushed the others aside. It glared at the boy lying on a floor of soggy sand, with nothing but a driftwood log as furniture in his new home.

'*A boy,*' said a teacher's voice. *'Nasty looking one, too. Class: all hoomuns are slow and their teeth are useless for biting and fighting. Write that down. Now!*'

Billy saw the sharks scribbling this in the sand with their fins. Gutsy was showing off: he used his tail instead.

'Write this as well: They are good to eat, except for the shells they make for their feet and body. Sometimes they have shells on their heads too, but those usually come off in the water.'

That day, every shark was allowed to "do an experiment" on Billy. Some scooped him out of the tank and chased after him until he ran out of air.

('Yeah, he's slow all right!')

Some tried to pull his shoes off, and finally one of them succeeded.

('His bottom shell tastes disgusting!')

Some tried to find out what he liked to eat.

('Miss! I've shoved lots of sea slugs in his mouth, but he keeps spittin' them out!')

Some wanted to know how high he could jump.

('Wow! When I poked him wiv dat electric eel, his head hit the top of the tank!')

Some drew pictures of him. Some measured him. Some weighed him. Some had a nibble when the teacher wasn't looking.

('Miss! Hammertooth's bit off one of his toes!')

Then they shoved some seaweed up into the tank and watched him fall asleep on it.

('Awww... ain't he cute? Can we keep 'im, Miss?')

The teacher put one big eye to the tank and smacked her lips. *'Yes,'* she said. *'He'll be safe here...'*

After a few days, Billy knew he wasn't safe at all. When

the young sharks went off for their lunch, the teacher would come up to the tank and whisper things like:

'Leg of boy with sea snail sauce on a bed of sea lettuce... Boy's head soup... Minced boy with sea lice... Oooh, dem crunchy ribs!'

This went on every day, and worse. They didn't know what to feed Billy so he had to live on sea slugs, jellyfish, sand fleas and bits of seaweed. The shark students sometimes played with Billy - but they weren't nice games.

'Hey, Gutsy — I got me dis sea snake. Let's make 'im fight wiv der boy!'

Or - *'Look, I found a prickle fish. We can take turns throwing it at him!'*

Billy had been a bully all his life and thought it was fun. But now he was discovering how horrible it was to be picked on. *(I would like to say that getting some of his own medicine made him a better boy. But did it? You'll have to wait until the end of the story to find out).*

A week later, during afternoon break, Billy was gloomily kicking the side of the Air Creatures Tank when he noticed something happening to one of the library displays.

A glass fronted door was opening. Then a tiny shape appeared from inside it, holding an shiny, silvery stick over its head. It edged cautiously across the sandy floor of the library. Billy thought it looked like the crab he'd tried to squash on the beach; and so it was.

The little crab saw Billy and swam up to the side of the tank. It looked in at Billy and nodded its tiny crab body. It clicked its claws at Billy, but kindly.

Billy shook his fist at the crab and shouted at it to *Go away!* The crab puzzled at him with its goggle eyes waving on their stalks. Then it tapped gently on the side of the tank with the tips of one claw.

Billy threw a shell at the tank side, startling the tiny crab. It looked at him, puzzled, clicked its claws but didn't swim away. Instead it raised its odd silver stick, which was as big as the crab itself. It tapped the stick on the tank's side. The tank shook, and rose a little from its shelf.

'What've you got?' asked Billy. 'A magic wand?'

The crab looked at Billy. It didn't understand him, but it waved the silver stick and the tank moved once more.

'Good crab!' Billy exclaimed. 'Do it again!'

The crab swam upwards, onto the top of the tank. Billy could see it walking above his head, to the end that was closest to the cave exit. It raised its little wand again…

… and the tank rose suddenly - and bumped against the roof of the cave, nearly flattening the poor crab.

The wand banged desperately against the top of the tank, and it dropped a little. The crab reached up a claw and rubbed the top of its shell, with a little crab frown. Then it pointed the wand forward.

The tank moved slowly out of the cave and began wallowing through the slow, cold waters towards the surface. Soon it was surrounded by sharks.

'Hey, Gutsy – ain't dat your hoomun?'

'Lost your boy, Gutsy!'

'Get 'im! Go on!'

The sharks slammed into the tank with their hard noses and sideswiped it with their tails. Billy was thrown about horribly, and every time he landed against one side of the tank he saw a big shark body coming at him.

But the tiny crab held tight to a clump of weed growing along the front edge of the tank and held its wand pointing steadily forward. Slowly, slowly they crept towards the beach and safety. The sharks shouted and banged on the tank and tried to bite it; but soon the water was too shallow for them and they had to turn back.

The tank was caught by the waves and slid onto the beach. The crab hopped off and struck the tank with its wand. The tank rolled over and Billy was able to push out the bottom panel. He fell out into the fresh air.

Billy stood up on the beach, a little shakily. The tiny crab looked up at him and clicked its free claw at the boy. In its other claw it held the silver wand.

This was Billy's chance.
He should have thanked the crab, shaken its tiny claw, and walked home. But he didn't.
'Give it to me!' Billy demanded, trying to snatch the wand. The crab began to back away.

'Give it to me *now!*' shouted Billy. The crab waved its free claw and scuttled off towards the water.

Billy leapt at the crab and stamped at it with one nasty, bullying foot.

He didn't have any shoes on – the sharks had eaten those – but his foot was big enough and tough enough to crush even the biggest crab. He smashed down *hard*.

'Owwwwww!'

Billy jumped around on the beach, holding his foot. The little crab watched him, puzzled. It reached up a claw and tried to straighten the wand, which Billy had bent when he stamped on it.

Billy sat down and looked at his foot. There was a red mark where the silver wand had been driven into his foot by the force of his own stamping…

…Actually, not so much a red mark – more a sort of golden orange mark. And the skin all around it was turning orangey gold as well.

'Owwwwww!' he complained again. 'Stupid crab! Look what you've done to my foot!' His foot was throbbing… it was going weak and floppy… his whole leg was floppy now… no – *both legs!*

He had a proper tantrum, kicking the sand and punching it with his fists. But his fists were floppy too, and then his whole body was floppy. And he seemed to be shrinking.

The tiny crab watched thoughtfully, with its shell tilted to one side. Billy shrank and shrank and flipped and flopped until he was nothing more than a small golden fish flopping about in the sand, gasping for breath.

The crab looked at him, thinking. Then it scuttled over to the empty tank and tapped it twice with the bent wand. The tank itself began to shrink and soon was no bigger than an ordinary goldfish bowl. The waves filled it with water and pushed it further onto the sand.

The tiny crab picked up Billy the Goldfish – not much bigger than itself now – and carried it gently to the goldfish bowl. It lifted the goldfish with its claws and stood upon its tiptoes - and then it heaved Billy into the bowl.

Then it picked up its silver wand again and ran happily to the water's edge. It turned to wave at Billy and clicked its little claws at him.

… Billy's mother was walking along the beach with her two remaining children.

'Hey – look, Ma! It's a fish tank!' said the boy.

'Can we take it home?' asked the girl.

Billy's mother picked up the tank. 'It's got a fish in it,' she said.

Billy the goldfish glared at the familiar face that was smiling down at him. He launched himself at it…

… and bumped his fishy nose against the bowl.

'He's a *mean* old goldfish!' said the boy.

'He looks like Billy!' said his sister. She put her finger into the tank and tried to touch the little fish. 'Ouch! He bit me!'

'He *acts* like Billy!' said the boy, with a laugh.

'We'll take 'im 'ome,' said his mother. 'We can call 'im Billy. After your bruvver wot's gone.'

The girl said, 'At least he won't pinch me like Billy did.'

'Or kick me.'

'Or bite the cat.'

'Or call us all names.'

Billy tried to say something rude to them, but since he was a goldfish, all he could say was 'Bwp Bwp Bwp…'.

'Awww, look!' said his brother. 'He's talkin' to us!'

'Ain't he sweet?' asked their mother.

And poor Billy had to put up with being looked after kindly for the rest of his life, with no one at all to bully…

… The crab however had many adventures with its magic wand. If you go to the seaside today, you might meet it dancing about on the sand, offering to turn you into a dolphin for a day…

If so, say "yes"…. *I* did.

Thursday Evening

At least they weren't underwater now. They were sitting on a deserted sandy beach, watching the sun go down. A warm breeze was blowing and somewhere an ice cream van was playing a happy song as it drove back to its own world.

A goldfish bowl sat on the sand, with a large, angry gold-fish swimming around in it, banging against the sides.

'Poor Billy,' said Brenda. 'I do feel sorry for him. Maybe if we return him to his home, he'll change into a nicer boy.'

She tried to stroke the back of the fish with her finger...

'Yowwwwww!' she shouted. 'He bit me!'

They put a lid on the bowl and set it into a box containing Grandma's wool and Robbie's book. Then walked up from the beach, looking for somewhere to stay for the night.

A sudden noise made them stop. One of those noises that most people can't bear to hear – a noise that when you do hear it, you feel you *must* do something about it.

A baby crying. Sadly, quietly. Crying without hope, crying from fear and hunger and misery.

Brenda strode off towards some bushes to their right, and the others followed. But the crying stopped.

Then they heard it up ahead, coming from a wood that was quickly going dark as the sun fell. They ran towards it and began poking about amongst the trees, but the crying came again, from further downhill this time.

'It's going towards the river!' shouted Tom. 'Quick! Before it falls in!'

Everyone charged down the hill, except for Wolfie. He sat back on his haunches, put his nose in the air and sniffed. Then he turned and trotted back to where they had first heard the baby. He lay down in the grass with his nose upon his paws and his ears pricked.

There were noises of people running about in the gathering darkness, calling to one another, 'Over here!' or 'I think I see it!' or 'It must have fallen down this well!'.

But Wolfie didn't turn his head. He just watched and waited. After several minutes, two grubby hands pushed aside a swirl of dried grass and a small, dirty, tear-stained face peered out cautiously.

'*Doggy?*' asked the baby girl, in a voice that trembled.

'Yeah, doggy,' said Wolfie. 'Sort of.'

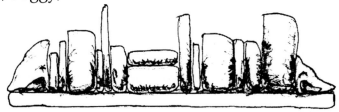

When the others returned after an hour of chasing shadows, they found the baby cuddled into Wolfie's warm fur, with its little head upon his chest.

'Shh!' he warned them as they started to talk. 'Don't wake her. She's had a hard time, this baby. She needs a good night's sleep and then some warm milk and toast.'

'Tom and I will go to the shops,' whispered Grandma.

'I'll build a fire,' said Robbie.

'I'll sing her a lullaby,' said Brenda.

... 'You see now?' asked Wolfie, the next morning. 'That was part of the Witch's horrible story. The baby would always be somewhere close, maybe only a few steps away, and yet she would never be found. Every time she thought she was about to be rescued, the person would walk right past her and go searching somewhere else.'

'But *why?*' asked Tom. 'Why would anyone do such a cruel thing to a baby?'

'Bad baby!' said the baby with a frown.

'You're *not* bad,' said Grandma.

'Shhhhhhhhhhh!' said the baby. *'Shut your cakehole, baby!'* Then it giggled and made a rude baby noise.

Everyone laughed except Wolfie. 'Poor kid,' he said.

'Put a sock in it!' said the baby. *'Button it! Shut your trap or I'll stick a slug in it!'*

'That sounds like Aunt Mildred,' said Robbie. 'Maybe the baby was being noisy. She would have told it to be quiet, and she would have been very angry when it didn't do what she said.'

'I'm warning you! Last chance for bad babies!' announced the baby, before biting happily into a piece of toast.

Wolfie shook his head and growled, 'When I see that Witch, I'm gonna rip her to shreds!'

'Before then,' said Grandma practically, 'we have to get to the end of the books. So let's think of a new story.'

'No tiggy,' said the baby suddenly, and began to cry. 'Want tiggy!'

'What's a tiggy?' they asked: but she couldn't tell them.

They put the baby on Wolfie's back and walked towards the woods. Before they got there, they came to a large oak tree with old, spreading branches. The baby looked up at the tree and threw herself off Wolfie's back. She began to crawl away at a great pace.

'Not fun!' she shouted. 'Bad tree!'

'Don't be silly,' said Brenda, scooping up the baby. 'It's only a tree.'

'Bite!' said the baby. '*Big* bite!'

'Trees don't bite,' Brenda said briskly. 'I'll show you.' She carried the protesting baby into the shadow of the branches.

'See?' Brenda said to the baby. 'Branches don't bite, leaves don't bite and I'm sure that the tree's *bark* is worse than its bite. And the little birds up there don't bite either. See? And that stripey cat thing won't... *Aiiiieeeee!*'

Brenda screamed and ran back towards the others.

'Tiger!' she shouted as she ran. 'In the tree!'

'Bite!' added the baby. '*Big* bite!'

Tom surprised them all by running out to Brenda and the baby, putting himself between them and the tiger-filled tree. Everyone stopped and stared at him.

'I thought you were afraid of everything,' said Brenda.

Tom look puzzled. 'I am,' he said. 'I sort of – forgot...'

Robbie said, 'Look above the tree.'

Ghostly words hung in the sky, like smoke rising from the branches: *Once upon a time there was a Bad baby. A Noisy baby. A baby that Wouldn't do what it was told. It made so much noise that it woke a tiger sleeping in the tree. The tiger opened its big, red mouth and showed the bad baby its sharp, white teeth. Then it leapt upon...*

'Run away!' shouted the baby. She wriggled free and began toddling back across the grass, falling every tenth step and crawling for a few moments before standing again.

Wolfie ran after her and sat on her the next time she fell over. He licked her face.

'*Bad* doggy!' the baby complained. '*Not* fun!'

'You just calm down,' said Wolfie. 'You're safe now. That tiger can't get you when I'm around.'

'Good doggy?'

'Yeah. Promise.'

Grandma sat with the baby in her lap while they discussed what to do.

'It's easy,' said Brenda to Robbie. 'Write a gun into the story, and we'll shoot the tiger.'

Tom asked, 'Can't we just turn it into a *kind* tiger?'

Wolfie growled, 'If you're gonna have a tiger in a story, it has to be realistic. You can't have a sweet, gentle tiger.'

'Exactly,' said Brenda. 'So we *shoot* the tiger.'

'No, we don't,' said Tom. 'We have a long talk with him and persuade him to become a vegetarian. No more babies for dinner, just pancakes.'

'Won't work,' said Wolfie.

'Bang!' said Brenda. 'Bang! End of problem!'

Wolfie said, 'No shooting either. I'm not having the baby grow up feeling responsible for killing an animal – unless we absolutely have to.'

'- Which we do!' shouted Brenda.

'No we don't,' Tom insisted. 'Anyone can change, even tigers. *Wolfie* changed.'

'- That's different –'

'- Bang!'

'- Pancakes!'

Robbie put his fingers in his ears and waited for the others to stop arguing. After the noise died down, he said:

'My mind is like a blank piece of paper. I've never had a brother or sister, or told a story to a baby before. I don't know what the baby would like... or do.'

Wolfie growled again; gently this time. '*I'll* do it,' he said.

'*You?*' asked everyone in chorus.

'Yeah. I've got an idea - it just came to me. *Don't* look at me like that! In fact, don't look at me *at all*. I can't tell the story with you lot gawping at me like a herd of tasty sheep. Robbie – got your pen? Okay, write this down...'

Good Puppy and Evil Kitten

The voices

The **Baby** is sooooo cute and sweet and simple. And she knows something that most adults have forgotten: that the whole world is there just for fun.

The **Good Puppy** is devoted to the baby. He too knows something that most adults have forgotten: that making someone else happy is just about the best thing *ever*. He makes puzzled noises at times, because he doesn't understand some of the baby's requests. He makes angry, growly noises at the cat, but puppy anger is rather cute and funny.

The **Evil Kitten** hisses when annoyed and snarls when *very* annoyed. He wants you to think he's a big tough tiger and not a sweet-looking kitty. He's very pleased with his evil plans, but he's rather bothered that the baby seems to like him - and he can't quite decide whether to be angry about this and bite the baby, or happy about it and purrrrrrrr.

The **Tiger** has a deep, rich, growly voice. He sounds big and warm and soft and furry and... very hungry. He moves silently: in fact, he's probably behind your chair or under your bed or behind the curtains *right now*, thinking 'Shall I eat the child now? Or wait until they've finished reading the story?'

The **Mother** is not a deep thinker. She spends hours talking to other mothers at the park but can never remember afterwards what anyone said. She always seems a little surprised when she looks down and sees that she's got a pushchair with a baby in it. She thinks the kitten is soooo cute and the puppy raaaahther naughty and the baby *ever* so sweet to have around, but... actually, where *is* the baby? Did she leave the baby on the bus again?

The story

Once upon a time there was a baby. She had no brothers or sisters to play with, but she did have a puppy with soft grey fur and yellow eyes.

The baby was just over a year old and she toddled about happily in her playroom or outside in the garden, with the Good Puppy always at her side or running off to fetch sticks, balls and toys for her.

One day they went to the park with the baby's mother. While the mother talked with other mothers, the baby sat in her pushchair and talked to the puppy.

'Want fun!' she said. 'Get me fun!'

The puppy looked at her with puzzled eyes. Then it ran off and returned with a stick.

The baby said, 'Not stick! Want *fun!*'

'Ruff?' said the puppy, which means "*There's nothing more*

fun than a stick, is there?"

The puppy dropped the stick and brought a soggy tennis ball instead.

'Yuk! Want *fun!*' the baby sulked.

'*Grrff!*' said the puppy, which means "*But tennis balls are fun! Especially wet, squashy ones!*"

The puppy thought hard. Then it saw a boy playing with a kite. The boy was laughing, so that *must* be fun…

The puppy ran off and returned with a stick, which had some string wrapped about it. There was a long line of string rising from the stick and disappearing into the sky: that was the kite string, still attached to the kite.

'*Good* puppy!' said the baby, watching the red kite racing from side to side across the sky.

But some other voices were shouting something quite different: '*Bad dog!*' And some big feet were running towards the puppy, the baby and the kite stick.

The puppy panicked and ran around the pushchair several times, wrapping the kite string about its wheels. Then it leapt onto the baby's lap and gave the stick to the baby.

'Fun!' shouted the baby. 'Fun!'

Just then a sudden wind caught the kite - and the pushchair took off like a racing car, bouncing across the park with a dozen children chasing it. The baby's mother stared as her baby zoomed off, making racing car noises.

'Neeeeeeeow! Vrrrrrmmmm! Vrrrrrmmmm! Fun!'

The pushchair was approaching a hedge at the end of the park… it was going at it very fast… it was going to crash…

'Neeeeow! Vrrrrrrmmmm! Vrrr… Help! Help! *Not* fun!'

'*Woof!*' said the puppy, which means "*Oh no! This is really going to hurt!*"

But it was too late to do anything… the pushchair was speeding towards the hedge… it got to the hedge… rose into the air … floated away into the sky.

'Fun?' the baby asked the puppy. 'Is dis fun?'

The pushchair spun around in the air, twice.

'Wheeeeee! Fun, puppy!'

The pushchair tilted until it was almost upside down. The baby was hanging by its straps, and the puppy was hanging on by its teeth.

'No! *Not* fun!'

'*Fwwf!*' said the puppy, which is the only sound a dog can make when dangling from a pushchair by its teeth. It means *"Help!!!!!"*

The kite pulled them up, up and away. Sometimes they were the right way up, but mostly not. Then the wind dropped and pushchair began to fall.

'Not fun…!' said the baby unhappily.

They were falling towards a large oak tree… the kite string snagged on a large branch… the baby's pushchair spun up and around the branch twice, and then swung to and fro like a big swing at a circus.

'Hooray! Dis fun!' the baby called as they swooped up and back. 'Do it again! Again!'

The puppy closed its eyes. It was feeling very sick.

'*Barf!*' it said, and you can guess what that means.

After a while the pushchair stopped swinging. The baby looked at the branches around it and then at the ground far, far below.

'Is dis fun?' she asked the puppy.

The puppy licked the baby's face, making her laugh. Then they heard a horrible sound…

… The sound of something large and cat-like… of something large and cat-like and hungry… of something that was vey angry at being woken by a baby.

The Tiger peered down at them from its place in the branches above. It began to make its way towards them.

'Nooooo!' said the baby. '*Not* fun! Bite! *Big bite!*'

The puppy closed its eyes and howled. The Tiger walked along the branch that the pushchair was dangling from and sniffed down at them. It spoke.

'Oh, *yum-mee!*' it exclaimed in a deep tiger voice. It reached down with a big paw and tried to fish the puppy up with it.

'*Barf!*' said the puppy again. '*Barffle!*' – which means "*I feel sick… I'm just about to be sick… I -*"

And then it *was* sick, all over the Tiger's paw.

The Tiger growled, 'How *disgusting!*' and wiped its paw on the branch.

The Tiger stuck out a long claw and began sawing at the string that held the pushchair to the tree. The string began to give. It broke. The pushchair fell. The Tiger leapt to the ground…

… a moment too soon. The puppy had grabbed at a branch with its teeth, and the baby had hugged the puppy tight. The pushchair dangled in the air above the puzzled Tiger, who was wondering where the pushchair was.

'Good puppy!' said the baby.

'*Fruff!* ...*Yowllllllll*...!' which means "*Thank you... Oh no I shouldn't have opened my mouth just then...!*"

The pushchair fell suddenly and landed on the Tiger's back. Its wheels wrapped about the Tiger's sides, so that it rested on the Tiger like a saddle.

'Grrrrrowwwllll!' exclaimed the surprised Tiger, who leaped into the air and then ran around the tree, bucking and snarling.

'Wheeeeeeee!' shouted the baby. 'Fun!'

'*Burffle!*' said the puppy, which means "*I've just been sick on the Tiger again!*"

The Tiger took off across the grass, bashing the pushchair against trees and biting at the pushchair's wheels. It came to the hedge the kite had flown over, and leapt back over it.

'There's the tiger!' someone shouted. A small white van began driving across the grass towards them. It had "Zoo" written on its side.

The Tiger turned into a play area beneath the shade of some large trees and tried to hide in the children's play-house there; but it couldn't fit inside because it had a push-chair on its back.

It jumped onto the slide, slid down it ('*Fun!*' shouted the baby) and threw itself onto a little roundabout which started spinning at great speed.

'Is dis fun?' asked the baby suspiciously.

'*Barf barffle burf!*' said the puppy, which means "*Look out, I'm about to be sick all over the place!*"

Men in white jackets jumped out of the white van, holding rifles loaded with tranquiliser darts. They ran up to the little roundabout just in time to be sprayed with puppy sick.

The roundabout slowed. The men in white jackets wiped the sick from their glasses and pointed their rifles at...

... at a puppy, a baby and a tiny, tiger-striped kitten.

'Oh.'

'Where's the tiger?'

'It must have run off into the bushes.'

'That way!'

'No – over there!'

'By the road!'

… and the puppy sick-soaked men ran back to their van and drove off.

The baby's mother came running up.

'My poor baby!' she exclaimed. 'Where have you been? I've been looking all over for you!'

'Fun!' exclaimed the baby. 'Stick no, ball no, kite yes yes up away wheeeeeee help help up wheeeeeee round and round and up and down and sick sick then *growl snarl bite bite* fall Yiiiiiii good puppy oooh down down wheeeeeee fun sick round and up like horsey zoom zoom wheeeeee den slide slide round and round *very* sick wheeeee!'

'Oh,' said the mother. 'I'm glad you had a good time…'

'Good puppy!' said the baby, hugging the puppy. 'Nice kitty!' she added, hugging the kitten - which tried to scratch the baby but the puppy bravely stuck his head in the way, and got its poor nose scratched instead.

'All right, then,' said the mother. 'You can keep the cute little kitten.'

'Hooray!' said the baby. 'Fun!'

'*Grrrrrr!*' said the puppy, which means "*Not fun!*"

'*Hissss!*' said the kitten, which means "*My evil plan is working!*"

The mother pulled the pushchair off the roundabout. 'What *have* you done to this?' she asked the baby.

The pushchair had one bent wheel and one wheel that had big chunks bitten off it. It had tiger tooth marks on the handle. It had kite string tangled around it. It had puppy sick all down the back.

'Fun!' explained the baby.

Evil Trick Number One

The baby was given a bath, which she loved. The puppy was given a bath and he howled all the way through it. The kitten was nowhere to be seen.

However, as soon as the baby and the puppy were alone for a few moments, the kitten appeared from under a sofa, hissed at the baby and whacked the puppy on the nose with a claw-studded paw.

'Nice kitty!' said the baby.

The kitten snarled, '*I'm NOT nice! I'm a witch's cat! I'm bad and a half! And I'm gonna teach you all a lesson!*'

The baby didn't understand any of this of course, and kept trying to stroke the kitten. The puppy however understood every snarl and mew.

'*Grrrffff! Yipp!*' the puppy barked, putting itself between the kitten and the baby – which means "*Be careful, baby! Danger! Evil cat! But I the good puppy will protect you!*"

The kitten laughed. '*No, no, little doggy,*' it meowed. '*You're the STUPID puppy who will get the blame for all my evil deeds!*'

'*Growlll!*' said the puppy, which means "*Leave the baby alone and fight me, if you're not a scaredy-cat!*"

The kitten laughed a cat laugh and then explained with a lot of hissing and mewling:

'*Nah. I've got a score to settle with you both. You see, after the old witch was turned into cookie dough, a magic spell gave me three Cat Changes. I used one to make myself into a tiger. You*' *forced me to use a second change so I could avoid being shot by the zoo keepers. You* **stole** *one of my magic changes! So I'm gonna make you both pay for that – and then I'm gonna turn my-self into a tiger again, eat you both, and escape again.'*

'Good kitty!' said the baby, giving it a hug.

'Nrrrrfff!' barked the puppy – which means *"No, he's not good! He's* **evil***!'*

'Hissssss!' said the cat, which means *"The good puppy's right for once!"*

'Love you kitty!' insisted the baby, giving the kitten a hug.

The bad kitten growled, arching its striped back. '**Nobody** *loves a witch's cat!'* it snarled. *'Not even the witch herself!'*

'Brff!' said the puppy, which means "For the first time ever, I agree with a witch!"

'Nice kitty!' said the baby, stroking it.

The next afternoon, the puppy was guarding the baby when they heard an urgent *Mew!* from the play room. The baby toddled off to investigate, though the puppy grabbed her dress between his teeth and tried to drag her back.

The playroom had a low table with a goldfish bowl on it, just too high for the baby to reach. The evil kitten had pushed the bowl so that it was hanging over edge of the table, and tilting towards the floor. The two goldfish were peering out nervously.

'Fishies!' said the baby, toddling forward and holding her hands out towards the bowl that tilted forward towards her… and then a little more…. The baby had almost reached the table and was reaching up above her head to touch the heavy bowl that was falling towards her…

The good puppy threw itself forward, knocking the baby aside and receiving the full force of the falling goldfish bowl on its own head.

The evil kitten laughed its evil, snarling laugh. It had given the bowl a little twitch at the last moment and sent it spinning, so that it landed on the puppy's head *upside down.*

The baby's mother came running to see why there was so much noise. She stopped, horrified at what she saw:

⚑ The howling baby was lying under the table, covered with water, sand, seaweed and fish food.

⚑ The puppy was running about the room with a goldfish bowl stuck on its head.

⚑ The kitten was nowhere to be seen…

⚑ … and nor were the goldfish.

'**Bad** puppy!' said the mother, taking the goldfish bowl off its head and whacking it softly on the nose with one finger. 'Look what you've done! *And* you ate the poor goldfish!'

'*Wff…!*' said the puppy sadly, which means *"I've been framed…!"*

Evil Trick Number Two

A few days later, the baby and the puppy found the kitten in the dining room. It was sitting on the table, eating cooked chicken off a plate that had been put out for the baby.

'Nice kitty!' said the baby, trying to pet it.

The bad kitten hissed. '*Look, kid – I've told you before - nobody loves a witch's cat!*' it snarled. And it went back to eating from the baby's plate.

'*Rrrrrffff!*' said the puppy. '*Bad cat!*'

The kitten smiled. '*Let's share!*' it replied. And it pushed the plate off the table, towards the baby's head.

The puppy jumped in front of the baby so that the plate bounced off its own head and crashed to the floor.

When the mother ran in a few seconds later, she found a terrible scene:

✓ The howling baby was lying under the table, covered with gravy and carrots.

✓ The puppy was standing next to a broken plate and some pieces of chicken, looking guilty.

✓ The kitten was nowhere to be seen.

'**Bad** puppy!' said the mother, hitting it gently on the nose with *two* fingers this time. 'Look what you've done! *And* you ate half the baby's chicken!'

'*Wffle…*' said the puppy sadly, which means "*I've been framed again…*"

But the worst thing was that the mother then said, 'Well – this chicken has been on the floor so I can't give it to the baby. I'll have to give it to…'

(The puppy looked up pleadingly at this point).

'…I'll have to give it to the *cat!*'

'Nice cat!' said the baby.

'*Howlllll!*' said the puppy.

Evil Trick Number Three

The next day started well, especially since the puppy was able to chase the evil kitten away from the kitten's own bowl and eat all its food, to pay it back for yesterday.

'I didn't want it anyway,' hissed the cat. 'I'm still full from my chicken dinner last night!'

But when the puppy and the baby took their usual walk around the downstairs rooms after breakfast, they found something odd. Very odd.

The baby's playroom had a large ceiling fan, which was only turned on in the middle of a hot summer. From its blades were hanging two long dog leads. The leads were fastened to a cushion, to make a swing seat at just the right height for a toddler.

'Fun!' exclaimed the baby, running forward and jumping onto the cushion. The seat swung back and forth gently. 'Play, puppy! Fun!'

The puppy looked about suspiciously. But there was no kitten to be seen or smelled, so he leapt onto the baby's lap and they had a wonderful time playing on the swing.

Then the puppy noticed that the swing was moving a bit faster than before… and faster still… and then so fast that it was too late to jump off.

The evil kitten was sitting on a high table next to the light switches. It had turned on the switch for the fan, which was now swinging the baby and puppy around the room in a wide circle.

'Meow!' it said smugly. 'I bet you're sorry now that you ate my breakfast!'

The puppy nodded. It really was sorry. The breakfast was swirling about in its tummy, faster and faster. 'Barf! Brfffff! Barrrfffllle!' – which means "I feel sick… I feel sicker… Oh no sicker than ever before!"

When the mother came running to see what all the noise was about, she was shocked to find:

☝ The baby was flying around the room on a home-made swing, shouting, 'Fun! Dis is fun! Wheeeeee! Helppppp!'

☝ The puppy was on the baby's lap, howling.

☝ A long line of puppy sick was being splashed on the walls, and then splashed on the mother.

☝ The kitten was nowhere to be seen...

The mother finally rescued the baby and the puppy. '**Bad** puppy!' she said, bopping it on the nose with *three* fingers this time, and not so gently as before. 'Look what you've done to the playroom!'

'*Wff Wffle Wooooooo!*' said the puppy sadly, which means "*I've been framed **again**... Bother!*"

The next week was quiet and the three of them even played some games together, which however always ended with the kitten stalking off.

'Love kitty!' said the baby, giving the kitten a hug.

The bad kitten snarled. '*No you don't! I told you - **nobody** loves a witch's cat!*'

'*I do!*' said the baby.

'*Frf!*' said the puppy, which means "I *don't!*"

Evil Trick Number Four

But one morning, the baby toddled into her playroom with her
puppy, and found the evil kitten
perched on the window ledge,
licking one paw and looking
very pleased with itself.

The window was never sup-
posed to be open, but it was
open now.

The evil kitten had lined up the baby's toys on the window ledge, and every few seconds it would give a toy a flick with its evil paw. The toy would rock forward and back, forward and back, forward and…

… and then it would topple out the window. A few seconds later there would be a thump or crash or tinkle as the toy hit the concrete far below.

'*Frppp! Grrrr! Drffff!*' growled the puppy, which means "*You **bad** cat! I'll get you for this!*".

A moment later, the puppy and kitten were rolling on the floor, biting and scratching. They were so busy fighting that they didn't see the baby toddle across to the open window and climb onto the window ledge.

The puppy was just about to bite off the kitten's left ear, and the kitten was just about to slice up the puppy's nose, when they heard the baby laughing from the window.

They froze. The baby was kneeling on the ledge and peering out the window. She leaned out and looked down at the concrete far below. She teetered on the edge. Her knees slipped…

The good puppy threw itself towards the window and managed to grab the hem of the baby's dress. But the baby was already falling and the dress ripped, leaving the puppy with a scrap of material in its mouth.

The evil kitten had run across as well, and leaped just as the dress ripped.

It leaped straight out the window, which was an odd thing to do…

… and its jump was more of a dive than a leap, which was even stranger…

… and the cat seemed to be trying to get to the ground first, which would have been the strangest thing of all…

… except that as it flew past the baby, it changed shape.

It grew wider and longer and softer.

Its evil eyes turned glassy and kind.

Its fur became fluffier than ever.

Its claws became floppy.

Then it hit the ground with a soft, heavy *thump*. And a moment later, the baby landed on it.

Up in the window frame, the puppy had his paws over his eyes. He took them off, one at a time.

The baby was lying on the soft, bouncy tummy of a large toy tiger. As the puppy watched, she sat up and laughed.

'*Fun!*' she exclaimed. '*Good kitty! Love Tiggy!*'

And the baby gave the big tiger toy a big hug.

After that, it was much more peaceful in the house. The witch's cat had used up all three of its Changes, so it had to stay as Tiggy the tiger toy.

If toys can be happy, Tiggy was the happiest of all. He was taken everywhere by the baby, hugged, cuddled and played with. He was allowed to join in all the baby's games, and at night he was tucked in next to the puppy.

And every night, the good puppy would say to the baby, '*Wufff!*', which means:

"I still say it's a bad cat!"

Friday Morning

They decided to wait until the next morning before Robbie added *"The End"* to last night's story. That way, everyone would get a good night's sleep first. They were woken by Tom with cups of tea for everyone. 'No slugs this time!' he promised.

'There's a beetle in mine,' Grandma pointed out.

'It's a very small one!' said Tom.

They packed their bags – mostly food but also the black book, Grandma's knitting, the baby's nappies and a goldfish bowl with a bad-tempered fish in it.

They decided to walk to the top of the hill and look around. But they'd hardly started when there was a shout from Tom:

'I'll save you!' … And they saw Tom throwing himself bravely between the baby and...

... a fluffy toy tiger.

'Tiggy!' shouted the baby. 'Found Tiggy!'

'So there *was* a tiger toy,' said Brenda.

'I thought I'd made it up!' said Robbie.

'You made up something that was already there,' said Grandma. 'It often happens that way, dear.'

'That was *so* brave of you, Tom,' said Brenda. 'It's a *very* dangerous toy!' Then she rolled on the ground laughing.

'It *might* have been a tiger,' Tom said. 'I was being careful.'

They added Tiggy to the pile of items they were carrying and climbed the hill. From the top they could look back along the route they had taken: just behind them, a grassy park; beyond that, a broad river leading to the sea; a forest beyond the river and castles beyond that, and more forest; beyond that, a blur.

Looking the other way, they could see very little: the land lay under a grey mist which veiled what appeared to be more trees and maybe another castle, far distant.

'What's ahead?' asked Brenda.

'Trouble,' said Wolfie. 'I feel it in my bones.'

'Scary things,' said a worried Tom.

'Run away!' shouted the baby.

'*Bwp*,' said Billy the Bully Goldfish, angrily.

Robbie said, 'There's only one way to find out.' He wrote in the book: '*THE END*'

… Nothing seemed to happen. After a few minutes they decided to carry on over the brow of the hill. Shortly after that, they entered the mist.

It thickened about them, cold and heavy like a damp overcoat. Soon they were blundering along little paths that pulled them deeper and yet deeper into the forest. Trees seemed to squeeze them from either side and step in behind them, blocking the way back.

'We should have marked our path in,' said Robbie. 'We'll *never* find our way out again!'

Tom groaned, 'Let's go back!'

'No,' said Grandma. 'We need to go forward. There's a book ahead, and children trapped in it.'

'What do you think, Brenda?' Robbie asked. 'Forward or back?' But Brenda didn't answer – because she wasn't there.

They tried several paths, shouting for Brenda. But then Grandma went a few steps into the forest by herself, and she didn't come back either.

An hour later, the fog cleared a little - and Robbie was all alone. He was just about to step out of the gloom into a patch of sunlight in front of him, when forty-two large teeth grabbed his leg.

'*Help! Hel-* ' Robbie began. 'Oh - it's you, Wolfie.'

'Yeah. Just you and me now. Hang on a second.'

They peered into the light. The trees formed a ring about a small grassy clearing. In the middle of the clearing was a house that didn't look right.

Wolfie sniffed. 'Gingerbread,' he said. 'Don't go near it.'

'Okay,' said Robbie. 'Let's go find the others instead.'

'They're inside,' said Wolfie. 'I can smell them as well. Let's wait a while and see what happens.'

They sat and watched. Presently the door opened a crack and a long nose poked out. Scary eyes peered left and right. The door shut.

This happened several times; then the mist swept in again and the house disappeared within it.

'Come on!' Wolfie whispered. They crept forward and crouched beneath a window, listening.

'How lovely for you to visit me, dears,' a very witchy voice was saying. 'When your friend comes, we'll have a party. Won't *that* be nice? Ah - but we'll need some party food and I don't have much in the cupboard.... *I* know! We'll have a nice pie to eat! *Baby* pie! Ha ha!'

There were some shouts and cries at this, and then the witch's voice continued:

'Mildred told me to expect some new guests soon, but I never guessed she would send quite so many. I *do* get tired of eating little Hansel and Gretel over and over again. Let's see: Baby pie for lunch, Tom pie for supper - you're called Tom, right? And when Mildred calls by (which she does every few weeks) I expect she'd like a bowl or two of Little Red stew....'

A new voice – a girl's - said bravely, 'Let them go! You've got *us*; you don't need anyone else, surely.'

'Oh, Gretel -'

'I'm *not* Gretel! You *know* my name is Gina!'

There was a slap.

'It's Gretel in THIS story! And your nasty little brother is Hansel!'

'It's Harry, actually,' said another new voice. *(Slap)* 'Ow!'

The witch's voice came again. 'The trees and the fog will

guide the boy here soon. It IS a boy we're missing, isn't it?'

'And a wolf,' growled a low voice in Robbie's ear.

The witch was clearly enjoying having an audience. 'Mildred and I go way back,' she said. 'We went to the same school! So when I got into a spot of bother with the police she says, Did I want to hide out in a book for a while? Only if it's a nasty one, I says, and she laughs like a drain and tells me it's Hansel and Gretel, so we both laugh like drains and then she shows me The Pen. Only two of them in the world, she says, and she's got them both. When the coast is clear and I come out again, she'll give me one of those, she says, because I've done her some favours in the past. *Witch* favours, I mean. Ha ha!'

'What kind are those?' they heard Brenda ask.

'Sharing spells,' said the witch. 'Lending poisons. Hiding bodies. But I must say, I'll probably owe her a few more favours after today. Three of you, all nicely tied up... plus the baby... plus Hansel and Gretel in their cage... and a goldfish. And one to come! Ah, if your parents could see you now, Hansel...'

'We don't have parents anyway,' said the voice of Harry, glumly. 'Only step-parents. And they would have sold us to you for a few pennies anyway, I reckon.'

'Not to *me!*' cackled the witch. 'To Mildred! She's the one who gets rid of unwanted children! Ha ha!'

Outside, Wolfie whispered in an angry growl, 'You wait here, Robbie. I'll go bite her legs off.'

'She'll have a wand,' Robbie warned.

'So? I've got something better!' Wolfie bared his teeth.

Robbie said, 'Okay.... You go, but try to get her wand first. While you're keeping her busy, I'll change the story. I don't have the book with me, but I don't think that matters.'

Robbie took out his pen and pointed it at the sky. 'Ready?'

'Ready,' said Wolfie, '- and armed to the teeth!'

'Go!'

H & G and the Witch's Cottage

The voices

Harry and Gina sound like the best friends you can imagine. They're funny, a bit cheeky, and easy to get along with. They're the sort of children who build a tree house in their garden and invite you over to play in it, pretending to be gorillas or Robin Hood or anything that's adventurous.

Their Step-Parents don't understand children, don't like children and sound really annoyed with Harry and Gina at all times, in all places and for no reason at all. They could remember the children's names if they could be bothered to try, but actually the only thing they care about is whether their favourite rubbishy programmes are on the TV tonight.
- Stepfather Three usually talks to the children in a jokey, pretend - friendly way but you can tell he might suddenly shout at H&G and give them a big slap for being cheeky, if they so much as look at him funny.
- Stepmother Four talks sweetly and enthusiastically most of the time, as if she's thrilled to have H&G around, but everything she says is *Nag Nag Nag* - unless she's talking to her friends about the children, when it's *Moan Moan Moan*. She gives H&G smaller slaps than Stepfather Three, but twice as many of them.

The Witch *almost* sounds like a dear, sweet grandma. But she tries too hard to make her voice appear kind and loving, and then she spoils the effect anyway by saying out loud the evil thoughts that suddenly pop into her evil head.

The Cat is totally confused. At the beginning, it snarls and hisses evilly because no one loves it, not even the witch of course. Then the children come and are quite nice to it, even when it's a hungry tiger. So now it doesn't know whether to bite or purr... bite or purr... oh all right, BITE!

The story

Once upon a time there were two twin children named Harry and Gina, called "H and G" because their step-parents couldn't remember their names.

Their real mother had died when they were tiny, and their real father had married Stepmother One. Then he ran away to Brazil, where he was eaten by pythons. Stepmother One married Stepfather One before leaving to live in Scotland, so Stepfather One got together with Step-mother Two – and so on. By the time this story starts, H and G were ten years old and already on Stepfather Three and Stepmother Four.

Their step-parents didn't really want children and moaned all the time at Harry and Gina, which was quite unfair because the twins did most of the cooking, all the cleaning and every bit of house repair. They were the only ones who knew how to work the remote control, change the batteries in the smoke alarm, start the lawn mower or build a new bookshelf.

The only birthday and Christmas presents they had this year were ones they bought for each other – but they were just what they wanted: matching toolkits, an electrical test-ing meter and ten vouchers each for the cinema.

Abandoned – take one

They knew something was up when Stepfather Three said at breakfast in a false, jolly tone: 'I know! I'll take you kids camping! Won't that be fun?'

Harry and Gina glanced at each other and said obediently,

'Yes, that would be *great!*' They knew better than to argue with Three. He had big hands and was a big slapper.

So as the evening approached, they were loaded into Three's pickup truck and half-waved off by Four, who was watching TV with one eye, listening on the phone with one ear and talking into it with her big mouth.

They drove into some nearby woods. Soon the truck turned off the main road and bounced through a maze of narrow tracks, its Satnav chattering instructions. Three kept looking across at the children and saying things like:

'You know not to throw anything out the window, don't you? No white pebbles or scraps of paper like the kids in that fairy tale. Don't do *this* sort of thing - ha ha ha!' He flicked his cigarette butt out through the driver's window, its bright stub bouncing into the dry grass.

'Of course we won't,' said Gina. 'That would be littering. And you might start a fire.'

'We wouldn't be able follow them back anyway,' said Harry. 'We'd have to throw one every few seconds to make a proper trail. We would need about 600 stones so far.'

'Yeah,' said Three. 'Not that you *will* need a trail, uh – '

'I'm Hippo.'

Three nodded. 'Yeah, I knew that. Hippo and um –'

'Giraffe,' said Gina.

'Yeah, that's right, Giraffe,' said Three. 'We're gonna have a great time, H and G. Family bonding!'

'Hope you brought a lot of glue,' said Harry.

Finally the pickup stopped in a small, damp clearing. Three unloaded two tents and set them up while the twins cooked sausages. Then Three told them boring ghost stories until they were so tired that they fell asleep.

They were woken in the middle of the night by the sound of the pickup driving away. Three's tent had gone, too.

Gina pulled a map from her rucksack while Harry took out his compass and a small wind-up light. They tracked across the wood, caught a bus and were home before dawn.

Three wasn't back yet, because his Satnav was taking him around and around the maze of tracks in the wood and he didn't get home until lunchtime.

Abandoned – take two

A week later, Stepmother Four suggested a Lovely Trip to the Wildlife Park.

'Of course, Stepmother,' the twins agreed. 'What a good idea!' They knew not to argue with Four either. She was a bit of a slapper, too.

The Park was a lot of fun until they got to the Lion Enclosure. Four's car rounded a corner and Four called out merrily, 'Look over there, um – Hannibal and – and -'

'Grapefruit,' said Gina.

'Yes – Grape, dear, look over there at the lions!'

As they turned their heads obediently, Four reached down and pulled at something. Then she stopped the car, exclaiming, 'Oh dear! That thing you put the luggage in – it's open! I can see it flapping! H and G, do you think you could just pop out and fix it? If you both lean on it together, that should make the lock catch.'

Harry and Gina exchanged looks again. They got out of the car and walked around to the back. The engine revved twice. The trunk lid clanged shut. Immediately, the car shot forward and sped away to the exit.

When Four got home, she picked up the children's bags from the rear seat, humming happily to herself. She went to put them in the dustbin but stopped when she heard a sound from the back of the car.

The car trunk opened and the twins climbed out. Gina tucked her screwdriver into a pocket and slammed the trunk shut again.

'We thought it would be best to fix the lock from inside,'

Harry said.

'Why, of course!' said Four. 'That's *exactly* what I thought you were doing. What clever children you are!'

She went into the house, slamming the door behind her. They could hear her shouting:

'Three! *It didn't work!*'

Really abandoned this time

A week later, a leaflet came through the door:
WHY CLUTTER UP YOUR HOUSE WITH THINGS YOU NO LONGER WANT? WE BUY OLD GOLD AND SILVER!
And in smaller letters it said:

PS - We also buy unwanted children!

'Yes!' shouted Stepmother Four, who showed it to Stepfather Three. And next Saturday morning...

'You're going to visit your grandmother,' said Stepfather Three at breakfast.

'*Step*-grandmother,' Harry corrected him. 'We only have step-grans, and there's about a dozen of them.'

'Thirteen,' said Gina, who liked to be precise.

'It's your Stepdad Two's Stepfather's second wife,' said Three confidently.

'No,' said Gina. 'She was the one who had ten pit bull terrier dogs. She fell down the stairs one day and broke her leg. *Bad* mistake! When the ambulance came, there was nothing left of her except a few bones.'

Four said, 'It's your third Stepmother's mother.'

'No, she was the one who sat in front of the TV all day eating the junk food they advertise. She exploded during a session of Jeremy the Broken Lie-detector,' said Harry.

Three shouted, 'Stop arguing! Enough of your mouth, Harvey! And you too, G-G-'

'That's right, "Gee Gee",' said Gina. 'I was named after a horse, remember?'

Three said, 'Yeah - I knew that! Now, you two toads are going to your Gran's for a few days. And *don't* ask me which one! Go pack a suitcase! *Now!*'

Harry asked, 'Just one case between the two of us?'

'I'm not sharing a case,' said Gina. 'It's unfair.'

'One case *each*!' shouted Three and Four together.

'Why didn't you say that to start with?' Harry asked.

'Get out of here!' Three shouted. 'Or you'll get a slap!'

Harry asked, 'Just one slap between the two of us?'

'I'm not sharing a slap,' said Gina. 'It's unfair.'

Then they ran upstairs before Three and Four could get up from the table.

They were loaded into the truck and driven far away by Stepfather Three – over high hills and then into a dark, eerie forest. The road shrank to a rutted track and snaked through the forest until it reached a tiny cottage hemmed in by mean-looking trees.

Three stopped the truck. 'Here's your Gran's house,' he said gruffly. 'Get out and fetch your bags.'

They pulled their small, wheeled cases across the mossy lawn,

bouncing over molehills and scattering small rocks. There was no path to the front door: as if no one ever went there, or perhaps did go in - but never came out again.

'It smells funny,' said Gina, wrinkling her nose at the cottage. 'Like old cake.'

'Gingerbread,' said Harry. 'And I can smell chocolate.'

The door certainly *looked* like a giant slab of chocolate, though if you tried to eat it, you would probably crack your teeth on the metal bolts that held it together.

There were tiny white dots on the chocolate door that looked like specks of mint but kept coming and going.

Harry caught one on his finger: it was a maggot.

The gingerbread walls were mouldy where they met the ground, and the sweets studding the walls had ants crawling on them. The sugar windows had attracted a lot of flies, most of which were still stuck to them. Large, grey slugs were licking the peppermint-stick window frames and wasps had made a nest in the frosted icing of the roof.

A too-sweet, too-friendly voice came from the other side of the stale chocolate door knocker:

'Nibble, nibble little mouse:
Who's that nibbling at my house?'

Gina replied:
'We didn't do it; we didn't get close.
We think your smelly house is gross!'

The door was flung open and a kind-looking grandmotherly figure stood just inside, holding a baking bowl which she was stirring with a big wooden spoon. She was wearing dear little granny glasses and her grey hair was tied into a granny-type bun.

'Do you like cookies?' she asked the children in a sugary voice, with a sugary smile to go with it.

'No,' said Harry quickly, because he was certain that any of Granny's cookies would be disgusting. 'They give me stomach ache and I end up groaning and howling all night long. You would need to wear earplugs and most of your windows would shatter from the sound.'

'Ohhhh...' said Granny, making a sad little face. She turned to Gina and asked, 'Won't *you* try some cookies, sweetheart? Just for me?'

'Cookies make me sick,' said Gina. 'I would be puking all

day and all night. You would have vomit on the floor and walls, and dripping out the windows. You'd be cleaning it off the ceilings for weeks!'

Granny glared at them and carried the cookie mixture outside. She used it to patch up one of the holes in the wall.

'What do *you* want?' she asked Stepfather Three crossly.

Three said, 'I – uh – you know – *brought your grandchildren to see you.*' He passed her the leaflet that had been delivered to the house.

Granny's voice went back to being sickly sweet again. 'Oh, the dear *grandchildren!*' she exclaimed. 'Come in, little ones. Now, let me see: can I recall your names, dears? No - don't tell me - it's been a long time but I'm sure I can remember!'

She peeked at the leaflet in her hand. 'Ah yes, it comes back to me! Little... G and dear H!' She looked at Three, who shrugged his shoulders.

'I'm G,' said Gina. '*Goudy Italic.*'

'And I'm H,' said Harry. 'Helvetica Narrow.'

Granny looked from one to the other. 'Perhaps you'd better bring your bags in,' she said. 'Then we'll all have a nice cup of tea and some cake!'

Overnight broom

'Cake gives me whooping cough,' said Harry.

Gina added, 'I can't drink tea. It comes out as fast as it goes in. From both ends. It splatters *everywhere!*'

Three said to the children, 'You kids have a good time with your Gran. Goodbye, uh –'

'Heartburn and Gallstones,' said Harry.

'Ginger and Horseradish,' said Gina.

Three scratched his head. 'Yeah. That's what I was gonna say. Bye then...'

He received a handful of banknotes from "Granny", climbed into his truck and sped off.

I'm a dear, kind old lady really....

'Now, my dears,' said Witch Granny. 'Come in and I'll show you around the house.'

She shut the front door behind them, locked it with a key and dropped the key into an apron pocket. She led them through the small cottage, with her evil-looking black cat growling behind them.

'Here's the kitchen... here's the toilet... here's the prison - I mean, *here's your room...* **my** room is at the end of the corridor and you must never, never go into it because if you do I'll have to cut out your eyes and feed them to the cat. Oops - just joking, ha ha! I'm a dear, kind old lady really....'

She laughed evilly – and her black cat meowed evilly, biting at their ankles. She led them back to the kitchen, which was also the sitting room and dining room.

'What would you like for dinner?' she asked. She had a nasty glint in her eyes.

'Nothing,' they answered. And they had a long, hungry, boring day while they waited for darkness so that they could escape. But as night blackened the smeared windows, Granny took out an old black book, put on her spectacles and peered at its pages.

'I'll read you a lovely bedtime story in your room,' she said in a sweet Granny voice. She snatched up their suitcases and led them into their bedroom.

It was an odd room, with a large bed in one corner and a big metal cage in the other - big enough for a dozen black cats, or two small children.

Granny threw their suitcases into the cage but left the cage door open. Then she placed her large backside firmly against the bedroom door and peered at her book.

She read very slowly:

> In cubiculum felix cattus
> Fiet tigris iratus magnus!

... And the cat turned into a large, angry tiger.

The children were chased around the room several times before they had the idea of leaping inside the cage and shutting the door.

'Good children!' croaked Granny. She came across with a key and locked them in the cage.

'And here's some lovely supper for you!' she exclaimed, pushing some revolting buns through the bars. 'Might as well fatten you up before I turn you into gingerbread! Oops - just joking, ha ha! I'm a dear, kind old lady really....'

They waited until the witch had gone to bed before taking their tool-kits out of the suitcases. They took the cage apart and cleverly rebuilt it around the puzzled tiger. Then they ate some food from their suitcases, threw Granny's buns to the tiger, and went to sleep in the bed.

When Granny came to wake them the next morning, she screamed.

'Good morning,' said Gina, yawning. 'I had

the oddest dream last night. The room turned inside out!'

'Yeah, I had the same dream,' said Harry. 'Then I woke up in this lovely soft bed!'

Growl! said the tiger from its cage.

'What about the buns?' Granny asked.

'Oh, *they* were eaten long ago.'

Growl! said the tiger again, looking rather sick.

'I must have done the spell wrong,' said Granny. 'You were supposed to eat the buns and turn into tasty little gingerbread children. Oops - just joking, ha ha! I'm a dear, kind old lady really....'

They had another boring day. Granny made them clean the entire cottage, including scraping green mould off the fridge and scrubbing out the toilet. They thought about escaping, but the tiger was always watching them.

While the twins worked, Granny peered at her book of spells and cackled to herself.

'I can turn your noses into snakes that eat your own eyes out!' she drooled. 'Or cover you with a thousand red ants! Just joking, ha ha!'

'Yes, that's a *really* good joke,' said Harry. 'What a great sense of humour you have!'

'Brilliant,' said Gina. 'How funny that would be, to have red ants stinging you all over!'

She and Harry pretended to laugh merrily. Then they asked, 'Can we go out to play?'

'Not until you've eaten your lovely, lovely raisin cookies!' Granny pushed a plate of cookies in front of them. She had that nasty glint in her eye again.

'I'm allergic to cookies,' said Gina. 'They make me cough and spit and sneeze. The snot flies *everywhere*! There would be absolute buckets of it dripping down the walls!'

'I'll eat them if you insist,' said Harry. 'But I warn you: raisins give me gas. *Lots* of gas. Last time, the whole neighbourhood had to be evacuated.'

The witch ground her teeth. 'What would you *like* to eat???' she screamed at them.

'Can we go out for a pizza?'

'No! You'll stay here until you're hungry enough to eat what I give you! And if you *don't* eat it, I'll use my nastiest spells on you and fill your knickers with scorpions! Oops - just joking, ha ha! I'm a -'

'- We know the rest,' said the children.

That night she locked them in the cage again. The children knew she would check on them, so they pretended to be asleep when she quietly opened the door an hour later. Then they leapt up and rebuilt the cage as before.

Next, Gina took the witch's spell book off the shelf in the kitchen and they set to work with a pair of scissors and some glue, moving the spells around and adding random letters to the words.

Evil Gran

The witch came in the next morning and screamed again when she found them sleeping happily in the bed, and the buns inside the tiger.

'Get up!' she ordered. 'I've had enough of being nice to you stinking brats!'

'Oh, goody!' said Gina. 'Nice grannies are *so* boring!'

'Can you be *Evil Gran* for a day?' begged Harry. 'Please?'

'And can you do some magic spells that actually work?'

'Yeah, *your* spells are sissy spells. They're rubbish!'

The witch stamped her foot. 'You've asked for it!' she shouted. '*Now* you're in trouble!'

'Hooray!' shouted Gina. 'We're in trouble!'

'Brilliant!' shouted Harry. 'I've always wanted to be in trouble!' The two children linked hands and began to dance about the room.

The witch's face turned red and she screamed at them, 'You horrible children! You pair of puking puppies! You slithering snakes! I'll teach you to make fun of me!' She ran for her book of spells.

'Which nasty spell should I do first?' she muttered to herself as she turned the pages.

'The one that turns someone's nose into a snake! *Please!*' begged Gina.

'Ha ha!' snarled the witch. 'Be careful what you ask for! Do you think I'm just pretending?'

'No,' said Gina. 'We just know you can't do it!'

'We think you're a *useless* witch!' said Harry.

The witch raged, 'You've had it! I'm going to make you wish you hadn't been born!'

The witch read out the spell, and it *did* work – sort of. Her *own* nose turned into a snake and kept trying to bite out her eyes as she frantically read the spell backwards to cancel it.

Harry asked, 'Isn't there one about turning the cat into an enormous scary spider, and turning a child into a fly for the spider to catch?'

'Yes!' cackled the witch. 'That's a good one!'

'Bet it won't work!' said Gina.

The witch stamped her foot. 'It will! It will!' she shouted.

'Won't!'

'Will!'

This time the spell *almost* worked. The tiger shrank to the size of a spider, but stayed a tiger. It was so funny to see him running about and making tiny tiger growls, that the children collapsed onto the floor in laughter.

The second part of the spell turned the witch into a tiny mouse, which the tiger then chased around in circles until the mouse made an enormous leap to avoid the tiger's teeth … and landed in a blender full of cookie mix.

'Shall I?' asked Gina, holding her finger above the 'ON' button. The mouse swam round and round in the sticky mess. It wore tiny glasses on its nose, which it just managed to keep above the thick, sludgy batter.

'Help! Squeak!' it pleaded.

'Better not. That would be cruel,' said Harry.

But just then the tiger leapt at Gina's finger to bite it, missed, and landed on the button. There was a *whizzzz* and the witch was gone.

'Oops…'

A week later they had rebuilt the cottage out of sturdy logs from the forest. They had to burn most of the witch's things, and took her bloodstained cooking equipment to the scrapyard. But they kept the chest of gold coins they found in her room.

Before throwing the witch's book of spells onto the fire, they turned the tiger back into a cat.

Gina said, 'Now kitty: you can stay with us or – *ouch!*'

The cat smiled and bit Harry as well.

'Okay,' said Gina. 'Maybe you'd better go. There's a spell here for witches' cats that are retiring. It says you get three cat changes. I don't know what that means, but it sounds better than the next spell, which turns witches' cats into a tasty cereal called Kitty Krunchies.'

She said the *cat changes* spell, and the cat hissed at her before running off into the woods.

'What shall we do with the gold coins?' asked Harry.

'We'll buy *lots* of vouchers for the cinema!'

'Bigger tool kits!'

'And we'll set up a playhouse for children who have step-parents!'

And that's exactly what they did....

Saturday

'That's *such* a sad story,' said Brenda, wiping her eyes. They were sitting around a picnic table outside the gingerbread house, eating cheese and tomato sandwiches in the morning sunlight.

'Why?' asked Tom, puzzled. 'Because the Granny Witch got whizzed to pieces in the blender? That was *great!*'

'Not that part,' said Brenda. She pulled her hood over her face, looking more than ever like Red Riding Hood. 'Those poor children. My stepfather… he was like that. But worse.'

'How much worse?' asked Grandma.

'A *lot* worse. Can't talk about it. That's why I eat so much. Eating is easier than talking.' Brenda lay down with her head in Grandma's comforting lap, and cried softly.

The others got up from the table and went to see what Harry and Gina were doing in the house.

'You attach the explosives *here*,' Harry was saying, pointing at one of the sugar candy pillars by the kitchen.

'No, we need to put them by the walls,' Gina insisted.

They were planning how to blow up the house, using some fireworks they'd found in the witch's bedroom.

'We could just knock it down by hand,' suggested Tom.

'Yeah!' exclaimed Harry. 'Sledgehammers!'

'Pickaxes!' shouted Gina.

Soon there was a demolition party at work on the house, using tools they found in the shed nearby. They worked away all morning and enjoyed themselves enormously. Even Brenda cheered up and swung an axe with gusto.

As the sun climbed to the top of the sky, Wolfie came out

of the half-destroyed kitchen with a plate of brown and pink cookies fresh from the oven, smelling delicious.

'Cookies!' he growled. 'Come get your Evil Gran cookies!'

'Lemonade!' added Tom. 'Made from real lemons!'

They sat down for cookies and lemonade.

'Delicious,' said Brenda, onto her second cookie already. 'I didn't know you could cook, Wolfie.'

'I can't,' Wolfie admitted. 'But there was already some cookie mix in the blender, wasn't there?'

Everyone stopped and coughed out a mouthful of cookies made from Evil Gran. They looked accusingly at Wolfie.

'Hey – it seemed a shame to waste it,' said Wolfie.

Six hands reached for six glasses of lemonade and began drinking. Six mouths spat it out again.

'Sorry about that,' said Tom. 'I suppose I should have used the inside of the lemons instead of the outside...'

Soon *THE END* was written in the book, which Robbie had found under Tiggy. They left the demolished house and walked for hours towards the castle. It seemed impossibly distant: days away, and they had only one day left.

As evening approached, they came to another cottage. Two large cars were parked outside it, and a small boy – perhaps two years old - was playing near the cars. As they watched, a man came out of the house and waved to someone inside it. The boy went up to him but the man pointed back towards the house, climbed into a car and drove off.

The boy wandered down the side of the house. Then a woman came out of the house. She peered about as if looking for someone, got into the second car and drove away.

The boy ran after the second car, shouting, but no one noticed. He ran back to the house, but the doors were locked and the windows were closed. He ran around the house

several times, then stopped and listened. He looked terrified. Then he sat down and put his hands over his eyes.

When the six (plus baby, goldfish, Wolfie and Tiggy)
reached him, he uncovered his eyes and stared at them.

'*Circus potty?*' he asked.

Brenda said to the others, 'He thinks we must be crazy
people who have escaped from a circus.'

'We look like it,' Wolfie laughed, coming out from behind
the others. The boy gasped.

'*Burrgle!*' he exclaimed and covered his eyes again.

The others looked to Brenda, who said, 'He's scared. He
thinks he's about to be eaten.'

Grandma sat on the ground and lifted the boy onto her
lap. The baby toddled up, dragging Tiggy. She peered into
the boy's frightened face and held out Tiggy to him.

'Hug!' she said.

The boy hugged Tiggy and looked happier. '*Home alone
better late never!*' he whispered.

Brenda said, 'He means that he's been lost here a long
time, but he's pleased that we've come at last.'

'*Gain again gone nitwits. Dark snarly burrgle!*'

'And,' continued Brenda, 'he says he gets abandoned by
his stupid parents over and over again, and then the scary
forest creatures get him each time.'

'You're good at translating,' said Tom to Brenda.

'My little cousin speaks *Baby Babble* too,' said Brenda.

Gina and Harry came back from a tour around the house.

'We can break in through a window,' said Gina.

'Let's knock the door down!' said Harry.

'Or climb down the chimney?' suggested Tom timidly.

Gina and Harry chorused, 'Yes! Like Santa!' They ran to
find a ladder, pulling Tom with them.

But Grandma was looking to the horizon, where the sun
was sinking fast. 'Maybe we'd better not wait,' she said.

'We won't,' said Robbie. 'Brenda – I'll need your help for
this one...'

The Wolf's Party

The voices

Daddy Human sounds as if he makes a lot of money "in the City". He carries a neatly-rolled dark umbrella which matches his dark grey suit. He is rather clever at work, and rather stupid at anything practical such as tying his shoelaces. He believes that it's Mummy Human's job to look after Baby Human on Saturdays, so he can go to the gym.

Mummy Human is one of those well-spoken ladies who like things to be neat and tidy. She's not particularly bright, and has to get out the cookbook every meal to remind her how to make porridge. She thinks it's Daddy Human's job to look after the little one on Saturdays, so she can go shopping.

Baby Human is a few months older than he was in the story "Mouldysocks" in Wicked Tales One. He's used to looking after himself, as well as finding the car keys for Daddy every morning and the cookbook for Mummy twice a day. He gabbles nonsense words in a most amusing little voice: but even so, he usually talks more sensibly than his parents.

Sir William Wolf is like all the other rich, self-important politicians you've seen on TV. His voice is deep and rather beautiful, and his words make pretty patterns in your head. But when he stops talking and gives you a big Politician Smile, you can't quite remember what he said, or how much it's going to cost you. He has a wonderful mansion with a moat, drawbridge, two-story duck house and a helicopter pad: all of which he claims on his expenses so that **you** pay for them instead of him.

The Pig has a slow, stupid and very friendly voice. He sounds puzzled by life at Miss Wolf's school, and wonders why there are so many cookery classes...

The story

It was Saturday morning. Daddy Human, Mummy Human and two year old Baby Human had just sat down for their breakfast (which was porridge - the only thing the parents knew how to make) when the doorbell rang.

'*Bah bding bdapppa rappa!*' said Baby Human, which means "I'll go to the door!"

'Oh yes...' said Daddy Human vaguely.

'Oh *no!*' said Mummy Human. 'Baby hasn't got any slippers on! What will the neighbours say?'

'Oh yes...' said Daddy Human. 'I'll go instead.'

'Oh *no!*' said Mummy Human. 'You haven't got a tie on! What will the neighbours say?'

'Oh yes...' said Daddy Human, looking down.

'I'll go,' said Mummy Human firmly.

'*Bah doopa wadda nibbles pray?*' asked Baby Human, which means "But what will the neighbours say?"

Mummy Human ignored him and went to the front door.

Daddy Human whispered to Baby Human, 'Why should the neighbours say anything?'

Baby Human whispered back, '*Bussa wassa nicka nockas!*' which means "Because she doesn't have any clothes on!"

Daddy Human looked down the hallway at Mummy Human walking to the door.

'Oh yes...' he said.

The door opened and then they heard Mummy Human scream, run to her room and start pulling on some clothes.

Daddy Human and Baby Human went to the front door. A large wolf stood there, wearing a fancy suit and a top hat. When he saw Daddy, he took off his hat and bowed.

'Good morning, my dear Humans,' he said, flashing his long, white teeth. His voice was deep and gentle and musical. 'I am Sir William Wolf, running for election. We in the Wolf Party would like to have your vote.'

He gave them a cheesy smile.

Baby Human asked, '*Wishy washy posh potty?*', which means "Will there be cake and ice cream at the Party?"

Daddy Human shook his head at Baby Human and said to the wolf, 'I apologise. He's just a baby, so he's *stupid*.'

Mummy Human came to the door (with her clothes on this time) and added, '- And he's a very rude baby, who *knows* he should say "Please"!'

'*Peas?*' asked a shocked Baby Human, which means "Yuk! Are we having *peas* at the party?"

'How sweet!' said Sir Wolf, smiling down at Baby Human

and patting him with a large, furry paw. 'I do **so** like little children.' He licked his lips once with a long, red tongue.

Sir Wolf took a piece of paper from his pocket and read out: 'The Wolf Party supports all children everywhere. Children are our **future**!'

'Oh,' said Daddy Human unhappily. 'But Baby Human here was born in the *past*.'

'Oh,' said Mummy Human unhappily as well. 'And Baby Human here is living in the *present*.'

Sir Wolf began to snarl but managed to control himself. He said, 'Children are our future **and** our past **and** our present!'

'*Creepa crawly piffle?*' asked Baby Human excitedly, which means "*Present!* Will there be presents at the party?"

Mummy Human glared at him, so Baby Human added hurriedly, '*Peas?*', which means "That would make up for having peas instead of ice cream!".

Sir William Wolf took another piece of paper from his pocket and read from it.

'Your vote is important to my Party. I already have:

The bat vote,
the rat vote,
the gnat vote,
even got the fat cat vote!
Got the votes of the dogs,
the hogs,
the fleas, flies and frogs.
I'm supported by the sows,
the cows,
the don't-know-whys and don't-care-hows.
We're loved by midges,
trolls under bridges,
the bugs that live beneath your fridges.
Spiders,
gliders
and broomstick riders!

'We don't have any support from the sheep, sadly,' said the

Wolf with a little smile and a lick of his lips. 'That's because those bad sheepdogs tell the sheep lies about us.'

'Oh yes…' said Daddy Human.

'*Bad* dogs!' said Mummy Human with a superior sniff.

Sir Wolf said, 'I would soooo like you to vote for me. When my Party gets into power, we'll make some changes that you'll like. For instance, we'll get rid of those naughty red squirrels that have invaded our countryside and stolen food from our beloved, natural grey squirrels, who are **much** more tasty – I mean, trustworthy!'

'Oh yes…' said Daddy Human.

'*Bad* red squirrels!' said Mummy Human.

'*Furry fibby flippy floppy?*' said Baby Human, which means "Isn't that the wrong way around?"

Daddy Human said to Baby Human, 'You *stupid* baby. Everyone knows that red is bad and grey is good! It's a scientific fact!'

Sir William Wolf patted Baby Human on the head with one big paw. His long, hard claws were rather scratchy.

'We're going to sort out the kittens too,' promised Sir Wolf. 'The mess they make! The noise! And what do they contribute to society? Nothing! While **you** are working hard at the office, **they** are lying about in the sunshine! So we'll make kittens illegal!'

'Oh yes…' said Daddy Human. 'What a fine idea.…'

'*Bad* kittens!' sniffed Mummy. 'Nothing but trouble!'

'Of course we'll vote for you,' said Daddy Human.

'You talk so beautifully!' sighed Mummy Human.

'*Budda creepy smugga snarla!*' exclaimed Baby Human, which means "But he's a *Wolf!*"

The Wolf smiled. 'Now then,' he said, 'You're just the sort of Humans I like. Why don't you come to the party at my house tonight? A **real** party this time, little Baby Human, ha ha! With cake and ice cream and lovely pork sausages…'

'Thank you,' said Daddy Human. 'That would be rather nice. It would make a change from porridge.'

'Oh yes!' sighed Mummy Human. 'I've always wanted to see inside Wolf Manor!'

'And you can bring stupid little Baby Human as well,' said Sir Wolf. 'My daughters and nieces will be babysitting any children who come. They **love** children!'

'*Burrgle!*' said Baby Human, which means "We're all going to die!"

The Party

At the party, Sir William Wolf met them at the door. He patted Baby Human on the head again and said to Mummy Human, 'My daughters run a little school in the west wing of the Manor. They're taking all the children there for party games. Would your little one like to go?'

'*Burrgle!*' said Baby Human again, and you already know what that means.

'That means he would *love* to go,' said Mummy, handing Baby Human to a lean, hungry-looking girl wolf.

'Gotcha!' said the girl wolf, dragging Baby Human down a long corridor before he could disagree.

She pulled him into a large room which had a writing board on one wall and some uncomfortable-looking chairs and desks stacked in a corner.

There were about thirty little ones running about the room, shouting and laughing – or squealing, squeaking, squawking or grunting, depending on what creature it was.

A pig came up to Baby Human. 'Duz you go to school here?' he asked.

'*Yukk!*' said Baby Human, which means "Yukk!"

The pig said, 'My mum sez it's a good school. My oldest bruvver went here. He liked it. But den he got lost on a school trip and didn't come back...'

'*Oh.*'

'Den my middle bruvver came here. He liked it too.'

'*Gainagain?*' asked Baby Human.

'Yeah, dat's right. He got lost on a school trip and didn't come back either. Funny, dat... innit?'

'*Innit,*' Baby Human agreed.

'I starts school here next week. I likes Miss Wolf and her sisters and cousins. But I ain't gonna go on dem school trips without takin' a map. No way!'

'*No way!*' Baby Human agreed again.

Just then they were called together for game of 'Pin the tail on the donkey', which everyone enjoyed except for the poor donkey...

... Then 'Pass the parcel', which everyone liked except for the squirrel which was wrapped up inside the parcel...

... Then 'Musical statues,' which was everyone enjoyed except for the hummingbirds, who fell to the floor each time the music stopped...

Now and then a door would open at one side of the room and a man wearing a white hat would look around, whisper something to a Miss Wolf and disappear again. A few moments later, one of the animals would be quietly led to that same door and pushed through it.

Meanwhile, Daddy Human and Mummy Human were having a good time eating, drinking and dancing. Then one of the other humans asked:

'Where's your little boy tonight?'

Daddy Human looked around. 'We must have left him at home,' he said.

'No,' said Mummy Human. 'He came with us.'

'Oh yes...' said Daddy Human. 'He must be around here somewhere...'

'Go check on him,' said Mummy Human, pointing to the far end of the house.

So Daddy Human wandered off. When he returned, he said, 'All the children are having a *great* time. They're playing some sort of fighting game. One of the pigs has been tied to a chair by the Miss Wolfs, and Baby Human is leading a pretend attack to rescue him. The children are waving sticks as if they were swords and throwing carrots at the wolves, who are snarling and pretending to chase them around the room. You should have heard the children screaming with delight!'

'What fun!' said Mummy Human. 'If Baby is having such a good time, let's have another dance!'

An hour later, Daddy Human was sent to check on Baby Human again. He was away for longer this time.

'Sorry, dear,' he said. 'I got lost on the way back. I looked in on Baby Human and he was having *such* a lovely time. The Miss Wolfs have made a little swimming pool out of an enormous cooking pot, and they threw the pig into it, but he kept squealing happily and trying to get out, and meanwhile the other children and animals were pelting the wolves with ice cream and jelly and shouting jolly playground things like *"Help!"* and *"Save me!"*. I didn't want to disturb their game, so I sneaked out through a side door.'

'I'm proud of you,' said Mummy Human. 'Other fathers wouldn't have been so thoughtful.'

Daddy Human continued, 'And then I realised I was lost, because just inside the doorway was a man wearing a tall chef's hat. I was in the kitchen of a restaurant! So I kept on going, and went out the front door of the restaurant. It's *such* a good idea – having a restaurant just behind the Miss Wolf School.'

'We must try it sometime,' said Mummy Human.

'Tonight's special was boiled ham.'

'My favourite!' said Mummy Human.

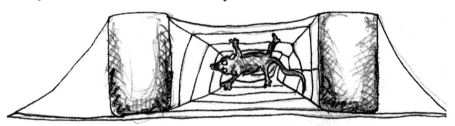

Half an hour later, a crowd of noisy children and animals came screeching and squealing and screaming down the long corridor. They ran onto the dance floor, calling and crying and carrying-on until their parents grabbed them, punished them for being so ill-behaved, and took them home.

A pig waved at Baby Human as he trotted off, shouting, 'Yay! We got away! Dat wuz fun! See you next time!'

Winter witch hat

Sir Wolf was at the main door saying goodbye to his guests. He looked gravely at Baby Human and asked, 'How did you escape the party – I mean, how did you *enjoy* the party?'

'*Rope,*' said Baby Human, which means "We

left your wolf children and nieces tied up and hanging up-side down from the ceiling by their toes."

'What did he say about rope?' the puzzled Wolf asked Mummy Human.

Mummy Human said, 'He said he loved every minute of the party!'

'If you had a good time,' said Sir William Wolf to Baby Human, 'why don't you come again? My daughters run a wonder-ful preschool class for tasty – I mean *talented* – little boys and girls. And they go on some **lovely** school trips: I expect you'd en-joy that.'

'*Burrgle!*' said Baby Human in horror.

'He keeps saying that word,' the Wolf said to Mummy Human. 'What does it mean??'

Mummy Human said, 'It means he'd *love* to come to school here!'

Sunday Morning

Robbie was all set to add *"THE END"* to the story when Brenda grabbed his hand.

'She's coming!' she whispered, and everyone froze.

They heard a door opening; footsteps; voices. It was Robbie's aunt and a man they didn't know.

'Here's my little library,' said Robbie's aunt. 'Not much to look at now, but it's growing all the time.'

The ten of them (if you include Wolfie and the goldfish) peered upwards. They couldn't see the room, just shadows swinging across the skies. Then a hand appeared; came towards them; touched the book they were in.

Robbie's aunt asked, 'Which would you like to hear? There's one about a child left alone at home...'

The other voice said something indistinct. The hand lifted and everyone breathed again.

'Or Red Riding Hood, maybe? That's always a favourite,' said Aunt Mildred.

'No!' whispered Brenda. 'She'll find out we're not there!'

They were relieved when the hand moved to the book just beyond theirs. Aunt Mildred opened it and laughed.

Witch hat with earphones

'Here they are – just where I left them last time. See? Boy and girl holding hands... girl just about to disappear (or should I make it the boy this time?)... long, painful hunt for one another... all ending in tragedy for them both. Ha!'

She read it in a chilling voice. When the boy fell off a cliff –

the girl screaming as she watched – the man clapped his hands as if he was applauding at a school play.

Aunt Mildred closed the book and placed it back on the shelf, her hand touching the book the children were in and sending icy shivers down their spines.

'Okay,' said the man. 'I'll give you fifty thousand for it.'

'No. Twice that, in cash,' said Aunt Mildred.

The negotiations went on for some time before they agreed a figure for the book. Then Robbie's aunt added:

'I have another nearly arranged; you may prefer that one. Come back tomorrow and I'll show you.'

'What kind of children?' asked the man.

Day at the races witch hat

'Oh, the *worst*! Cheeky, with dirty hands and big laughs. I've had my eye on them for weeks. When they checked out their books on Friday, I thought *I'll have you!* They took out the book I hate the most: it's called *Wicked Tales Three*. Books One and Two were bad enough!'

The witch seemed to be peering towards the children on the shelf; or perhaps towards the unfortunate new children she was going to snatch on Monday.

'They're reading *Wicked Tales Three* right now,' she gloated. 'And I've got my eye on them... Ha!'

Once the door had been closed, and the house had fallen silent, Robbie wrote *THE END* with a hand that shook.

The boy and girl were just as the witch had described them at the start of the story she'd read: sitting on a park bench, hand in hand. The boy looked scruffy; the girl was dressed in the sort of clothes you normally see on models, though her designer dress was ragged and tattered now.

Everyone exchanged shy hellos – or *'Yellow!'* from the toddler.

'You must be the child from the story next to us,' said the

girl, looking at him. 'The one we call *Burrgle* Baby because that's what you say the most.'

She had a precise, clear and superior voice that made her sound a little stuck-up. But she also had a lovely smile, and Burrgle Baby immediately went to sit on her lap.

'*Bongoman,*' he said.

'Benjamin, I think he means,' translated Brenda.

The new girl said merrily, 'Bongo Burrgle Baby!' - and that's what the toddler was called from then onwards.

The new boy said, 'I'm Davy,' and shook hands with everyone. He had very rough, strong hands. 'This is Anastasia. She's a princess – a real one – well, she *was.*'

Princess Anastasia also shook hands with everyone and tried to learn their names. 'Davy and I have been friends for ages,' she said. 'But my parents didn't like me seeing friends that weren't rich and "properly brought up" as they called it. So we used to meet in the park... and then we started meeting in the library. *Bad* mistake!'

'*Burrgle!*' agreed Bongo Burrgle Baby from one knee.

'Yuk!' said Baby Girl from the other.

'We can guess the rest,' said Tom.

'We heard her reading the story she's put you in,' said Wolfie. 'She's a nasty piece of work, and no mistake.'

'But you're going to let us all out, aren't you?' asked Anastasia. 'We've heard your new stories, every day this week. We were surprised that the witch didn't hear them as well.'

The others gasped.

'Was she in the room?' asked Robbie.

'At least twice,' said Davy. 'Maybe more than that.'

'She can't have heard us,' Brenda said. 'Otherwise...'

'*Endofstory!*' said the toddler.

'Not fun!' said the baby.

'Robbie,' said Grandma: 'I think we're in a hurry.... *I'll* tell this one quickly, if you'll write it down.'

Biker witch hat

Davy and the Trolls

The voices

Davy talks sensibly at all times. He usually has a bit of a laugh in his soft, musical, country-boy voice, because he really enjoys forest life - even though it's sometimes dangerous.

Princess Bossyboots starts off sounding ultra-posh and... well... ultra-bossy! But after sharing a bowl of soup, she eases off the bossiness: you could call her Princess Bossyslippers now. Her voice is the opposite of Davy's: smooth where he's rough, precise where he's relaxed and thoughtful - but you can tell she finds him amusing. She does scream and cry rather desperately when the trolls are making their nasty plans, but you and I would probably do the same.

Her father the **King** has bossiness and rudeness multiplied by a hundred, then squared, then built into an enormous concrete castle and dropped on your toe.

The **Crabs, Foxes, Snakes and Bats** don't say anything at all except for the clicks, yaps, hisses and squeaks you'd expect.

The **Trolls** are the stupidest creatures imaginable. They would spend all day watching TV, if only they could figure out how to turn it on. They are also the most evil and bloodthirsty bunch of thugs you'll ever meet... and if you **did** meet them, that would probably be the last time you met anyone in this world.

The **Mother Troll** is slightly less stupid than the others, which is why she's allowed to use the frying pan.

The story

Once upon a time there was a boy named Davy. He had no family and lived in the forest.

The forest was the best place in the world, and he was never bored. He made a hut out of branches covered with moss, which kept him warm and dry.

He lived on nuts and berries and a wonderful forest pea

soup he'd invented. He never ate the forest animals because that would be like eating your next door neighbours. Instead, he spent hours watching them and copying their voices. He could mimic every bird and could copy most other creatures too – foxes, mice, hedgehogs, badgers and even the happy otters that splashed in the river.

He went to town once a week to swap nuts and berries for bread and potatoes and sometimes a bit of bacon, because he loved bacon sandwiches.

The Princess and the Pea... Soup

One day the Princess came into the forest with the King and Queen and a lot of fancy people. They rode around on noisy horses, with even noisier dogs running in and out of the trees chasing the foxes and anything else they could find. They spent the whole day hunting animals and then didn't even take home most of the dead ones.

Davy hid quietly in his tiny hut, where a pot of forest pea soup was bubbling gently. He knew that if he wandered out, the dogs would chase him and a Lord or Lady would send an arrow after him, laughing.

He was reading a pirate story called *The Game of Pirate* when he heard a loud knocking on his door.

It was the Princess. She was only about his age, twelve or so, but she was bossy enough for twenty.

'What are you doing in this forest, boy?' she demanded. 'This is my father's forest! He'll have your head cut off!'

'That's just silly,' said Davy. 'I've never hurt him.'

'But it's HIS forest!' the Princess shouted. 'I'll tell him!'

'Then you're as silly as he is,' Davy said. 'Would you like some pea soup?'

'No!' said the Princess. 'You aren't allowed to offer me food. You're just a common boy and I'm a Princess!'

'Okay,' said Davy, smiling. 'Don't have any, then.'

The Princess sniffed the air. The soup smelled delicious.

'However,' she said, 'I can *order* you to give me some soup, and I will: Boy, give me a bowl of soup. *Immediately!*'

So the Princess had two bowls of soup while Davy read her a chapter of *The Game of Pirate*. She said it was the best soup she'd ever had, and the best story she'd ever heard.

'Boy!' she said. 'I've changed my mind! I *command* you to stay in this forest! And you must always give me a bowl of soup when I ride through!'

'Yes, Princess Bossyboots.'

'*And* you must read me a chapter of a book!'

'Yes, Princess Bossyboots.'

'Don't call me that!'

'I won't, Princess BB.'

The Trolls

One night the boy woke - and was suddenly very afraid. There were noises outside that didn't sound right.

Big noises...

UGLY noises...

TROLL noises

He huddled down beneath his feather-stuffed quilt. Hill trolls are **bad** news. They only come out after dark because of a skin condition they have, called *Photopetrogenesis...*

... in other words, their skin turns to stone in sunlight.

To start with, only the skin of the troll changes, so that the troll is trapped in a rocky shell. Then the troll turns into a stone statue very slowly, from the outside inwards.

But *please* don't feel sorry for hill trolls. When they aren't wandering about at night looking for children to eat, they're at home planning ways to catch children or their pets. They like puppy pie and kitten casserole and hamster hotpot and deep-fried bunny with mushroom sauce almost as much as they adore chocolate-coated children. They are mean and stupid and very, very greedy.

They're also great cooks, but that's no excuse.

What happens to trolls that have turned to stone? They end up in parks or museums. People find a stone troll on a hillside, drag it to the city, mount it on a slab of stone, and then invent a story about it. You'll see something like:

Field Marshall Sir Rotgut Custard 1800 – 1850

Fought bravely in the Slob War and defeated Slug the Terrible

But what the inscription really means is: *We found this statue in the woods and didn't know what to do with it, so we stuck it in the park.*

If you don't believe me, go find the nearest statue. Have a really good look at the face. That's a troll, isn't it?

Davy knew it was a troll crashing about the forest because of the smell. Hill trolls don't wash. You can smell them long before you can hear them! And because of all the dirt, no one knows what colour trolls are. You would have to scrape off a lot of dirt before you got down to skin level, and no one has ever done that. We may *never* know.

The good thing about Troll Stink is that they can't smell anything themselves, so Davy was safe so long as he was quiet. He breathed very lightly, knowing that trolls have excellent hearing. Finally the troll sloped away towards the lights of the city.

Davy was worried, though. The next morning he built a new hut deeper in the forest but left a note on his old hut for Princess Bossyboots to read the next time she visited.

Little Girl Lost

When Davy went to the city to swap berries for bread a few days later, he told everyone about the troll: but no one believed him.

'Trolls are just a fairy tale, young man!' said the baker's wife, passing over two fresh loaves.

'I only believe in what I see,' said the butcher as he handed over the bacon, 'and I've never seen a troll.'

So Davy shrugged his shoulders and turned to go back to the forest, when a trumpet was blown and everyone had to stop and listen to a royal announcement:

The Princess has disappeared! Anyone who has seen the Princess yesterday or today, or knows anything about where she is, report it immediately! Reward offered! The Princess has disappeared! Anyone....'

Davy almost dropped his shopping. There was only one thought in his head: **the Troll.**

He ran to the Palace and told the soldiers standing at the gate. They laughed and poked him with their spears. He pushed past them into the Palace itself, and was chased all the way to the King's throne room. He threw himself at the King's feet and told the King about the troll he'd seen, and his fear that the troll might have taken the Princess.

The King said, 'What a *stupid* idea! The Princess never goes into that part of the woods by herself!'

'But your Majesty,' said Davy, 'maybe she was on her way home from hunting and decided to visit me in my little hut. She usually does that on Fridays. Then perhaps the darkness fell sooner than she expected.'

The King sprang to his feet and shouted, '**What???** You've been speaking to the Princess alone? And without my permission??? Guards! Seize this boy!'

Someone said, '*He's* probably the one who took her, your Highness. You can't trust common boys.'

'Yes!' shouted the King. '*He* must have done it! Take him to prison and poke him with something sharp until he tells us where the Princess is!'

And so poor Davy was marched through the streets to the prison. He knew that once he was in prison he would never get out, so he waited until the soldier's hand on his shoulder relaxed its cruel grip just a tiny amount, and then he ducked, dived and dodged for his life through the twisting alleys, jumped over a wall and ran into the forest.

Lost as Well

The soldiers chased him deep into the forest, and he spent hours dodging from tree to tree. Day turned to night and he was sure he had escaped; but then he heard the dogs.

When the King's hunting dogs caught something, they liked to rip it into tiny pieces: though if they were in a good mood, they just bit its legs until the hunters came with spears and poked it full of holes. Davy didn't fancy either of those, so he fled wildly into a part of the forest he'd never explored. He scrambled onward for hours.

Finally he stopped, realising that he was completely lost; lost in the middle of the night. The moon rose as he came to a path that ran towards some low hills. The path looked as if it had been trampled by very heavy feet...

He turned left and followed the path until it stopped at the mouth of a large cave. He sniffed.

Trolls!

He hesitated. He heard the dogs howling, closer now.

'I'll be safe from the dogs... but the trolls might get me... *but* I might find the Princess,' he said to himself.

The thought of the Princess pulled him into the cave. It was black inside, so he took a candle from his pocket and lit it. He made his way forward, step by careful step. It was a high cave, with a floor that had been pounded smooth by heavy footsteps but which had many cracks and holes that a boy might twist his ankle in.

He hadn't gone far before he came to a hole on the left side. He peered through it and saw a family of foxes peering back. The father and mother foxes growled at him.

Davy made gentle fox noises back and said, 'It's all right, Mr and Mrs Fox. I won't hurt your babies.'

The parent foxes nodded their heads and stopped growling. Davy gave them bacon and bread, and they licked his hands, which is how a fox says "*Thank you*".

A few minutes later, he came to a family of snakes slithering up and down the cave walls. The father and mother snakes hissed at him and showed him their poisoned fangs.

Davy hissed back in a soothing, musical way. 'It's all right, Snakes,' he said. 'I won't hurt your babies.'

The parent snakes nodded their heads and stopped hissing. Davy gave them some bacon and bread as well, and they dipped their heads three times, which is how a snake says "*Thank you*".

Several minutes further along, he came across a family of large crabs that clambered out of the cracks in the cave walls and snapped their claws at him, angrily.

Davy held his hands in front of him and clicked his fingers in time to a pleasant crab tune he knew. 'It's all right, crabs,' he said. 'I won't hurt you.'

 The crabs stopped trying to pinch him. Davy gave them some bacon and bread, and they waved their claws about in circles, which is how a crab says "*Thank you*".

And then he heard something terrible.

It was a distant sound, and not at all loud. But it made him start running as fast as he could manage with a flickering candle in his hand.

It was the sound of a child crying out in fear. When Davy heard it, he wanted to run away because he was afraid, too.

But he knew that voice - so he ran *towards* it instead.

'Prin- !' he began. But he stopped halfway through the word and slowed to a quiet walk. He whispered: 'Princess, I'm coming – but I'm coming slowly and quietly because I mustn't let the trolls hear me.'

He crept along the dark, smelly passageway for several minutes before he heard that cry again, somewhere close by. He blew out the candle and put it in his pocket.

He tiptoed along, feeling the wall with his hands. Then he stopped: *There!*

His eyes had grown accustomed to the darkness now and he could see the outline of a doorway in the rock just ahead, on the right hand wall.

There was no door in the doorway; it was just a stone arch that opened into a flight of steps leading down and around to the right. Somewhere at the end of those steps was a flickering light that cast enormous shadows upon the dull stone walls.

Then he heard voices. Troll voices.

The Frying Pan

'I say we eat her now!' said a deep and stupid voice. 'Cos I'm hungry!'

'Stupid trollock!' said a higher voice. There was the sound of metal hitting something slightly softer.

Whangggggggg!

'Ouwwwwwww!' said the deep voice again. 'Dat hurts!'

An even higher voice said, 'You've dented the frying pan! Ma, you've dented the frying pan!'

'Yeah,' said the deep voice. 'Why'd you do dat?'

The second voice - the voice of "Ma" - said, "To shake up your stupid brains! You know we can't eat her yet! Not till we've got what we want!"

Davy had been creeping down the steps and now he peeped around the edge of the stairway. A rather nasty sight was waiting for him.

An enormous woman troll was standing by the kitchen fire, facing Davy. She had a frying pan as big as a car wheel in one hand, and was trying to get a dent out of it by punching it with a large, hard fist.

To her right was an even larger troll, who was rubbing the top of his head and glaring at her. Beyond them was a small boy troll who was pinching something in a chair just out of Davy's sight, hidden behind the bigger trolls.

The mother troll saw what the boy troll was doing and shouted, "How many times have I told you? Don't play with your food!"

And she gave him a wallop on the head with the frying pan as well.

Bongggg!

The boy put his hands on the top of his head and groaned. "I didn't touch her!" he lied.

Davy moved a little further down the stairs and could now see a small figure seated in a chair large enough for the boy troll. She had golden hair and was trembling with fear. There was a rope about her chest, tying her to the chair.

'Please let me go!' begged the Princess. 'I'm sure my father will give you a reward.'

'Dat's right,' said the father troll. 'A BIG reward. Dat's the plan!' He laughed nastily - and then burped nastily as well.

'Manners!' shouted his wife and clonked him on the head again with the frying pan.

Thwannnggg! 'Owwwwwwwww!'

'Huh!' she said. 'Think yourselves lucky I'm not going for your noses with this!'

The hands of the other trolls immediately flew up to their noses to protect them.

'Idiots!' she said. 'I said I WASN'T going for them!'

The hands went down, very slowly.

'The nose is the only bit dat's soft on me,' said the father troll.

'And me,' said the boy troll.

The mother troll said, 'Stupid trollocks! It's the only soft bit on ALL trolls!'

'Oh yeah. I was forgetting,' said the father troll. 'Now - when do we get a bite of the Princess?'

Bonnnnngggggg! The frying pan did its job again.

'Ohhhhh....' said the father troll. 'Now I remember. We ain't gonna eat her yet. You're gonna take a piece of her back to the city, and you're gonna tell the king... um... I can't remember dat bit.'

The mother troll said, 'I'm going to tell the king he's gotta send us fifty children to eat - nice plump ones. Then he can have his precious Princess back!'

'Awwww!' whined the boy troll. 'I don't want to send her back! I want to -'

Whannnnnggggggg!

'Shut your mouth!' said the mother. 'Of course we ain't gonna send her back! That's only what we're gonna tell the king!'

'Oh...' said the boy troll. 'Dat's a GREAT plan!'

The father troll said, 'But which bit of her are you

gonna take to the city?'

'Easy,' said the mother troll. 'I'll take a scrap of her pretty dress... wrapped around one of her pretty fingers!'

The Princess cried out in fear again. Then she started shouting at the top of her voice, 'Help! Help! Somebody please help me!'

'Stop that noise!' shouted the boy troll. 'I don't like it! Stop it!' He put his hands over his ears.

The mother troll gave the frying pan to the father troll, saying grimly, 'It's YOUR turn to use it!' She pointed at the girl.

The father troll looked at the frying pan, puzzled. He thought hard about what to do with it and then...

Whanggggg!

... He hit the boy troll on the head with it.

'No!' shouted the mother troll. 'Don't hit HIM!'

The father troll thought hard again and then...

Bonggggg!

... He hit the *mother* troll on the head with the pan.

'No!' shouted the mother troll. 'Not ME neither!'

The father troll looked even more puzzled. He thought hard one last time and then his eyes brightened and...

Whanggggg! Bonggggg!

... He hit *himself* on the head, twice.

A Cunning Plan

Davy had been searching about on the staircase for something and now he found it: a smooth stone, about the size of an egg. He weighed it in his hand, waiting for the right moment.

The trolls were arguing now about who was going to cut off the Princess's finger, and they were all looking at the poor girl.

'YOU'RE not doing it!' said the mother to the boy.

'Chopping off fingers is a grown up thing!'

The boy crossed his arms and turned away, pouting.

'STUPID OLD TROLL!' said a sulky boy troll voice from somewhere.

'What did you call me?' shouted the mother troll, grabbing the boy troll.

'Me? I didn't say nuffink!' said the boy. 'It was Daddy!'

'You can't trick me! It was YOUR voice!' said the mother troll. 'BAD trollock child!'

Whangggg! Wallopppp! went the frying pan.

'Owwwwwww!' went the boy troll.

The mother troll turned back to look at the Princess again - and a rock caught her right on her big nose.

'STUPID OLD TROLL!' said the voice as the rock hit her.

'Ohhhhhhhh my nose!' she screamed. 'You BAD boy!'

Bonnngggg! Whack! Kerpowww! went the frying pan.

'Go to your room!' she shouted, and pushed the boy troll down some stairs at the far end of the kitchen. Davy could hear the boy bumping and banging as he bounced all the way down the stairs to the caves below.

The mother troll gave the father troll a *wife* look. 'It's YOUR fault,' she said. 'You're always spoiling him!'

Then she turned back to the girl. 'Give me your hand!' she commanded. She took a knife from the kitchen table.

A low troll voice said, 'It's not MY fault, you old witch! The boy takes after YOUR stupid side of the family!'

She whirled about. 'What did you say?' she demanded.

The puzzled father troll said, 'I didn't say nothing. YOU said it!'

'It was YOUR voice!'

'Wasn't!'

The mother troll raised her frying pan, but the father troll had grabbed a teapot from the table.

'I'll break your best teapot!' he warned. 'Put down dat pan or I'll smash the teapot to smithereens!'

'All right,' said the mother troll. 'But you'd better leave my teapot alone. It was my Gran's.'

She put the frying pan on the table and turned to grab the girl's hand again.

The low voice said, 'I hated your Gran anyway!'

A second stone flew through the air - and the teapot shattered in the father troll's hand.

The mother troll whirled about again, and for a moment the two trolls stared at each other in fury. Then they both snatched up frying pans and saucepans and rolling pins and hammers and clubs and began walloping each other for all they were worth.

Just as the battle started to quieten down a little, a boy troll voice seemed to come up from the floor below, saying, 'Na-Na-Na-Na-Na! I've flushed all your favourite things down the toilet!'

The bigger trolls looked at each other and then flung themselves down the stairs, shouting and punching and walloping as they went.

Whanggggg! Bonggggg! Owwwwwww!

Unexpected Help

Davy slipped into the kitchen and snatched up the big knife. He cut through the ropes that held the Princess and pulled her out of the chair.

He stopped a moment to light his candle in the fire, and together they ran up the stairs and out through the doorway at the top.

They ran as fast as they could without putting the candle out. Behind them, there were muffled thumps and yelps from the trolls' cave. And then they heard the mother troll's voice, very loud and clear:

'Wait a minute! .... We ain't GOT a toilet!'

Then they heard heavy footsteps stomping up some stairs and then some angry shouts... and *more* footsteps up *more* stairs and then along the tunnel.

'After her!' the trolls were shouting. 'Catch her! Kill her! Eat her alive!'

Davy and the Princess ran as fast as they could, but trolls can run much faster than humans: and soon there were three huge shapes looming up behind.

Davy came to the place where the crabs lived. They slid out from the cracks and waved their claws at him, but in a friendly fashion this time.

'Help me, please!' said Davy.

The father crab turned its eyestalks towards the large, dark shapes approaching, and nodded.

Davy whispered as he passed, 'Go for their noses!'

The crab clicked its pinchers to say "yes' and began scuttling up the rocks, followed by all its family and friends – twenty big crabs and a hundred little ones.

The trolls stomped closer shouting, 'There she is!'

'No – There THEY is! Two of 'em now!'

'Get 'em!'

'Yeah – Owwwwwwwwwwww!'

'Owwwwwwwwww!'

'Owwwwwwwwwww!'

Why the cries of great pain? The crabs had dropped onto the trolls' heads and were merrily pinching away at three soft noses. As quickly as the trolls brushed them away, more crabs dropped from the ceiling to take their places.

Davy and the Princess ran as quickly as they could, and it looked as if they would get away – until Davy tripped, the candle went flying, and his ankle went *crack*.

'Keep going!' Davy gasped. 'Just head for that gleam of moonlight! You can do it, Princess! It's not far!'

But now it was the Princess who was brave. She pulled Davy up and supported him along the rocky path.

They couldn't go fast and soon the trolls were puffing and panting close behind them. But then a snaky head popped up in the darkness and hissed at them.

'Please, Mr Snake,' pleaded Davy. 'Help! Get their noses!'

The snake nodded his head three times and turned to hiss to his family and friends. In moments, the whole snake tribe had wriggled into the cracks of the cave floor.

The greedy trolls came stomping along the cave.

'Dere dey is!' said the father troll.

'There dey ARE, you mean - you stupid trollock!' shouted the mother.

'Dere WHO is?' asked the boy.

There was a pause for several thumps and punches, then the trolls started running again.

'I see 'em!'

'We gonna get 'em!'

'We gonna - OWWWWWWW!'

'Yiiyiiiiyiiiiiiiiiiiiiiiiiii!'
'Oh my poor nose!'
'And mine!'
'I think mine's broke off!'

Fifty snakes had leapt up and wrapped themselves around the trolls' legs, so that they tripped and fell nose first to the ground. Then – as the trolls rolled on the ground in agony – snake heads would pop up for a moment, bite any noses nearby, and drop down into the cracks again.

Davy and the Princess continued their slow hobble towards the cave entrance. It was hard enough for Davy, with a broken ankle: but think how hard it was for the Princess, who hadn't slept for two days and hadn't eaten for three. Yet she trudged on, holding Davy up.

The cave entrance was coming, but not quickly enough. Soon they heard the shouts of trolls once more; soon they smelled them; soon they knew the end was near...

They came to the family of foxes and even before Davy could beg for help, the mother fox had yapped to her friends and family. A dozen foxes crept along the walls of the cave and waited.

As the trolls stormed around the last corner, foxes jumped up at them, biting, snarling, yapping, scratching.

'My nose! I gotta fox on my nose!'
'I got one as well!'
'I got two of dem!'

And as the foxes were knocked aside by the angry trolls, their place was taken by hundreds of bats returning from their nightly feasting. The trolls had to wade through a sea of creatures that sang and squeaked and yapped; that nipped noses, pinched ears and bit bums.

Photopetrogenesis

Davy and the Princess had got to the very end of the cave now. They were exhausted, and fell to their knees. But it was no good. Behind them they heard the trolls forcing their way outside. Davy and the Princess turned their heads and saw the triumphant monsters running towards them. The children tried to crawl further; they could not.

'Dere dey is!'

'ARE!'

'I see 'em!'

'I gonna bite the boy!'

'Me first!'

'I gonna eat the girl!'

Bonnngggg!

'Silly trollocks! Not yet!'

'Owwwww – I'm gonna eat one leg anyway!'

'Owwwwwwwweeee – And I'm gonna eat the other!'

'Get 'em!'

'Get 'em!'

GET –'

And then there was silence.

For it was dawn and the first rays of the sun, those sparkling rods of light which bring life to all good creatures, turned the trolls to rock in mid-leap.

Three stone statues fell heavily to the ground next to the children, and stayed where they fell.

Later that morning, two ragged children limped up to the palace and tried to go inside. They were of course snatched up by the guards and taken to the royal prison.

After many hours, someone realised that the very dirty girl really *was* the Princess, so she was set free. And then she shouted and threw things at her father the King until he agreed to release Davy as well.

Davy's ankle was better after a few weeks and he went back to his little hut in the woods. The King invited him to come live in the palace, but as Davy pointed out:

'Thank you, your Majesty. But I think I'm safer with

wolves and trolls than I am with you Royals.'

And though the King didn't much like it, the Princess spent most afternoons in the woods and often took her other friends with her.

... And if you want to see the three stone trolls, go to London and take a look in the big gallery of Modern Art there. Someone has put different descriptions on the three ugly lumps of stone that some people call "Art", but you and I know what they really are.

The Final Book

'I'm afraid,' said Brenda.

They were standing at the edge of the forest, looking into a cave entrance that led inside a steep, rocky mountain.

'I hope we don't have to go in there,' said Tom.

The newest children went forward and peered in. Davy said, 'There's a light coming from somewhere. Maybe the cave goes all the way through the mountain.'

Anastasia gave him a playful push. 'You're supposed to be brave,' she said. 'Go investigate!'

Davy laughed and tried to push her inside instead. '*You're* the brave one, not me! Robbie got that part all wrong.'

Robbie meanwhile was puzzling over the black book. Every time he tried to write "*THE END*", it disappeared.

'We can't have got to the end of the story yet,' suggested Wolfie. 'Follow me!'

Wolfie padded into the cave, followed by the others. It was just as Davy had thought: after about ten metres, the cave swung to the right and they were out again. But not into another forest: *into a lighted room.*

It was a pleasant room in some respects: high, broad, with big windows along one side looking out onto a lawn and tall trees. The walls were lined with shelves and every shelf was full of books.

'We're in a library.'

'And there's the librarian.'

They all looked towards the librarian's desk, then turned and started to run back to the cave. But the cave had vanished; it was now a wall of books.

The Librarian beckoned to them. They went, dragging their feet. The baby began to cry and the toddler covered his eyes, muttering, *'Burrgle! Gainagain nastyhag!'*

Robbie's aunt was writing in a large black book. They crept up to the desk and tried to read what she was writing.

'This is the eighth book,' she said. 'I'm getting it ready for tomorrow. But first I need to finish off the book you're standing in. It won't be a *happy* ending, I promise!'

She looked at them, one by one. They said nothing.

'Did you think I didn't know?' she asked. Her voice was sharp now. 'Did you think I was blind, deaf and stupid? Oh, you thought you were being so clever. *That* made me laugh! It almost made me puke too, because I had to listen to all your stupid stories. They were *useless!*'

They still said nothing.

'Well, all your pathetic fairy tales have come to nothing. I'm sending you back - all of you! You'll return to your hideous nightmares – they'll never end – they'll get *worse* – and I'll do a new one for Robbie: the Snow Queen. How'd you like to spend the next hundred years shivering, with splinters of glass in your heart, hey? *Answer me!*'

Grandma took up her knitting again. 'You can't make us go back,' she replied calmly. 'And I'm warning you: you'd better not try. You don't know what you're up against.'

'**What?**' shouted Aunt Mildred. 'How *dare* you lecture me? I invented you! You and that stupid wolf didn't even exist before I wrote Red's story!'

Grandma turned to Robbie and said with a smile, 'She invented something that was already there. Happens all the time, doesn't it?'

Robbie laughed – and then they all laughed, which did two things: it seemed to break some sort of spell; and it made his aunt furious.

'That's enough!' the witch fairly screamed at them. 'I won't have this kind of behaviour in my library!'

She snatched up her pen and began to write, in dark jagged letters than almost tore the paper in her black book:

And then the children found they were back –

But Robbie had opened his own book, and when his aunt paused for a fraction of a moment, he wrote quickly:

- back in their own –

The same words appeared on both pages, as if they were two screens showing the same movie.

He was about to write "*homes*" but the witch leapt in with "*stories*" and screeched triumphantly, but too soon because Robbie added some words while she was exulting:

- stories except that they were now good stories with happy endings which took them all the way to the final book and then –

He hesitated for a tiny, fatal moment.

'Ha ha!' the witch screeched as she plunged her pen onto her own page:

- and then the witch KILLED –

They all knew what she was going to write, and there wasn't going to be a pause. They were about to die.

Grandma had been watching carefully, even though half her attention seemed to be upon her knitting.

- and then the witch KILLED -

A knitting needle stabbed across the table, into the witch's hand. At the same time, forty-two wolf teeth bit her leg.

'Owww!'

The witch dropped her pen and - quick as a flash - Brenda put her hand over Robbie's own hand and wrote:

*- killed **herself** -*

And even now Robbie paused, not wanting the add the punctuation mark that would make it final.

In front of him, his aunt was staring at the book, her face pale, her features twisted with shock and rage.

Around him, the others were jubilant. But their joy turned to horror when she added some words:

- killed herself a million years later.

Robbie was frozen with disappointment. He couldn't think what to do. His hand trembled. The children all stared at the two books, their hearts pounding.

The witch added, without any rush, as if she knew she had won:

Until... then... she... -

But an idea came to Robbie, from nowhere, and he wrote:

- she slept.

There was a long pause. They all looked at the face of the witch. Her eyes were closed but she seemed to be fighting against the spell. Her hand began to write very slowly, as if in her sleep:

S...h...e... -

Grandma took the witch's pen and finished the sentence:

She wrote no more but slept soundly, with good dreams, for a million years. And the moment she woke, she died.

Robbie offered his snake pen to the others, and Tom took it. He added:

A few minutes after she fell asleep, the others escaped from the final book.

Gina and Harry fought for the pen next and decided to write the next sentence together:

And they were best friends after that, forever.

The pen was passed back to Robbie. He was about to put in the final two words that close a book when Grandma said, 'Just a moment, Robbie. Wolfie and I have something to tell you.'

'What?' they all asked.

'Yeah,' said Wolfie. 'We didn't want to say until now.'

'We're not coming with you,' said Grandma.

'What??' they asked again.

'They would put me in a zoo,' said Wolfie.

'And I wouldn't have any grandchildren to look after,' said Grandma.

'You'd have *us!*' said Brenda – and they all agreed.

Grandma nodded. 'Yes, dears – and I'm sure Wolfie and I will find a way of visiting you all from time to time.'

'Yeah,' growled Wolfie. 'I'll jump out from the shadows and give you a fright!'

'Our place is here,' said Grandma. 'From here we can visit the sad children, the lonely ones. I can be their imaginary Grandma and Wolfie here will make them laugh.'

Wolfie added, 'Yeah. Got some good stories to tell them. And some tricks to show them, too.'

It made sense, somehow...

'Now,' said Grandma, 'there are some things we ought to agree before you go. Robbie, you need to throw that pen on the fire as soon as you get to the other side.'

'Yes, Grandma.'

'And you've always wanted a sister, haven't you?'

Robbie nodded. He didn't think anyone knew.

'Brenda's going to move in with you.'

'I am?' asked Brenda, her eyes suddenly bright.

Robbie thought of all their arguments – and then of all the things they'd done together.

'You are,' he said to Brenda. 'That is – if my father and mother agree – and if my mother....'

'That will be all right,' said Grandma firmly. 'Your mother is much better. The witch lied.'

'What about us?' asked Gina, Harry and Tom together.

'I expect you'll spend most weekends at Robbie's house!' laughed Grandma. 'As will the others.'

'You can all come to my castle every other weekend,' said Anastasia. 'If my father complains, I'll throw things at him!'

Grandma continued, 'It may take a few days to work out where the baby and Bongo came from, but you'll manage. And I'll take Billy the goldfish back to his own house.'

'I'll look after him!' said Wolfie, with a wolfish grin.

'No you won't!' said Grandma, poking him and laughing. She looked at the others. 'Goodbye, dears,' she said.

There were a lot of hugs and tears.

They left the witch snoring, with her head on the desk. Grandma and Wolfie left quietly by a side door, carrying the goldfish bowl. The others walked to the main entrance; the large wooden door was locked but they knew what to do. Robbie took out the pen and added the final words:

And they were best friends after that, forever. THE END.

And it was true: they *were* all best friends after that, forever.

Some other books by Ed Wicke for ages 8 and over...

WICKED TALES   Nine crazy stories. Did you know that the bears think *Goldilocks* is a stupid story and have their own version? Or that lightning is made by a family of trolls living in the clouds? What happens when Alicroc the Alien becomes a teacher at a nursery school? How does a dancing horse save a fairy from a witch? Why does Snow White team up with the 7 Easter Bunnies, and why do they have machine guns?

WICKED TALES TWO   Chock full of crazy characters. Gangster rats and a cute baby... Jack, the Giant, the Ogress, the cow, the magic chicken and the magic hat... Alicroc the Alien scoutmaster... The Bad Tooth Fairy, the Tooth Mice and the Toenail Fairy... The Gorilla tricks the Hunter, with help from a Singing Snake... Cinderella, the Fairy Grotmother and the 6 Easter Bunnies clean up at the Palace!

BILLY JONES, KING OF THE GOBLINS   Billy Jones has the same sort of problems you have – a grandma who's loopy, a school bully who wants to thump him, and a mean teacher who insists he'll have to do the school's country dancing display dressed as a girl! But on his tenth birthday he's woken at midnight by a group of weird goblins who tell him he's now their king. You *know* it's going to get crazier by the minute...

AKAYZIA ADAMS AND THE MASTERDRAGON'S SECRET   A school visit to London Zoo causes Kazy Adams to swap the rough streets of London for a new world of magic, adventure and danger. And in Old Winsome's Academy, there's an ancient mystery to solve: the disappearance of nine pupils during the Headship of the Masterdragon Tharg, at the time of the Goblin Wars.

AKAYZIA ADAMS AND THE MIRRORS OF DARKNESS   The second adventure of Akayzia Adams and her friends starts with one mirror and ends with another. In between, there are three worlds of magic, a squadron of werewitches, a fistful of trolls, and one annoying little lizard with a taste for chocolate. And in the Academy, there are thousands of spiders... some of them not spiders at all.

MATTIE AND THE HIGHWAYMEN   It's 1845. Recently orphaned and running away from her bullying aunt, 13-year-old Matilda Harris finds herself down in The Devil's Eyeball with an eccentric, well-spoken highwayman; his gang Lump, Stump, Pirate and Scarecrow; and two young "brats" who have escaped from the notorious Andover Workhouse.

BULLIES   The only book in the world with a fairy who conducts anti-bully warfare using beetles, a snowman that talks in riddles, a school assembly taken by a talking bear, a little sister who starts a pirate mutiny at school and a boy who turns into a bird after Christmas lunch! A book packed with poems and riddled with riddles. A book that's serious about bullying... but *crazy* about everything else!

NICKLUS   There's a mad scientist who wants to destroy all the cats in England, and nobody can stop her – except Nicklus and Marlowe. Nicklus is a nine year old boy who hardly talks at all. Marlowe is a talking cat, the "coolest cat in England". Together they set out on an adventure to find Nicklus' missing mother and save the cats.

Lightning Source UK Ltd.
Milton Keynes UK
UKOW040943210213

206612UK00002B/12/P